Escape From The Billings Mall

A Select Your Own Timeline Adventure

CHUCK TINGLE

DEDICATION

To all those who make this timeline the beautiful place that it is.

HOW TO READ THIS BOOK:

Welcome to The Tingleverse, a place where unicorns, bigfeet, dinosaurs and living objects are a typical part of our daily lives. This reality is similar to the one that you're currently reading from, but positioned on a slightly different timeline.

Every action you take, or don't take, creates several new timelines of reality. These worlds have been blossoming into existence since the universe began, and will continue until it ends. It's a power that we all have, but rarely know we're using.

This book will illustrate just how important making choices can be. Unlike most books, which are read chronologically from front to back, you read a Select Your Own Timeline book by following the instructions in italics at the bottom of most pages. If there is only one option, these words will inform you which page to turn to next. However, there will often be multiple choices that you, the reader, get to select on this important journey.

These forks in your journey will look similar to this:

To order the spaghetti, turn to page 1325
To order the chocolate milk, turn to page 7489
Leave the restaurant on page 3244

If there are no words in italics at the bottom of your page (or story ending), it is assumed you should continue reading onto the next chronological page of the book, as you normally would.

Throughout your Tingleverse journey, you will sometimes find an item that you can carry with you. It's important to remember the items you've collected, so using a piece of scrap paper to write them down as you go might be helpful, though not required. When you receive an item, it will be written in all capital letters LIKE THIS.

The only other time you will see something written plainly in all capital letters is if you reach the end of a particular timeline path, and thusly the end of your story. It will be written as THE END.

If you come to a path that explicitly involves an item you don't have, you cannot take this path. If you cannot remember whether or not you possess an item, then it's assumed you do not. In this case you lost your item or left it somewhere along your journey.

Sometimes, a specific path you take will cause you to lose an item. If an item is lost, it will be written in all capitals and italics, *LIKE THIS*. Sometimes, instead a specific item, you will lose *ANY ITEMS* you are carrying.

If you ever return to the first page, you will automatically lose all of your items.

Now that we've covered all the rules, please enjoy your journey through the various timelines of The Tingleverse! Your tale begins on page one.

It's been a long day in Billings, but there's one very important stop left on your list. You're headed towards the mall in search of a gift for your son, as his 25th birthday is, technically speaking, just hours away.

Obviously, this is something you should've taken care of weeks ago, but it's not like you haven't been trying. Your son means that world to you, and his birthday is not an event that you'd soon forget. The real issue is in the fact that he's become nearly impossible to buy for.

In his younger years, the things that your son was interested in were fairly easy to track, and it made the world of holidays and gifts incredibly simple to navigate. Long, long ago, there were entire years when all he cared about were fire trucks. Later on, his attention moved on to playing the guitar.

Now that he's in his mid-twenties, however, your son is capable of going out and getting himself anything that he wants. The threat of buying him something that he already has looms large in the back of your mind. His interests have also evolved, becoming more and more abstract and difficult to nail down.

Your son loves technology, he loves reading, he loves sports, and he loves dressing well for work. These are all categories with a lot more breadth than his previous interests.

Thankfully, it's the thought that counts, and you know this truth deep down in your bones. Your son will appreciate anything that you get him, and he loves you no matter what, but that still doesn't keep the stress from mounting.

You've let this gift giving anxiety suffocate you for much too long, not exactly sure what moves you should be making and therefore making no move at all. Now, there's only a single evening of shopping left, and you intend to make it count.

That is, of course, if you can get to the mall before things start to close.

You glance down at the clock in your car as you swiftly cruise the roads of Billings, pushing your speed just a little bit more than you probably should. The sun hasn't yet set, but it's right on the verge.

Long shadows stretch out across the road like stripes as you drive, casting the scene in a glorious orange glow that would probably be something worth taking in and meditating on, if not for the fact that you're running dangerously low on time.

2

Instead, you focus on the road ahead, your eyes locked on the streets before you in a state of deep intensity. You're on a mission.

Your heart racing, you realize that a slight mental detour is in order while your hands and eyes do the dirty work. After all, a watched clock never strikes, and there's still a couple of minutes left before you'll be pulling into the mall parking lot.

The thick forest of deep green trees continues to whip past you on either side of the road as you reach out and turn on the radio. There are few options to choose from.

To listen to The Snow Channel, turn to page 32
To listen to Billings Action News, turn to page 5
To listen to The Top Pop Hits with Brindle Creems, turn to page 81

It's a long trek through the vent, with several vertical climbs that force you to push yourself tight against either side and then slowly, gradually hoist yourself inch by inch up the metal tunnel. By the time you get to the top you're utterly exhausted, but as you start to feel the cool night air against your skin a second wave of energy floods through your veins.

You finally reach the top and discover a thin metal screen blocking your path. Fortunately, it only takes a few swift kicks to bust out the flimsy covering.

You climb out to find yourself standing on the roof of The Billings Mall, a seemingly endless cascade of stars above you and the moon illuminating everything from high and bright in the sky. In other circumstances, this would be a glorious Montana evening, but today is not like other days.

You make your way over to the edge of the rooftop and cautiously gaze down over the side, gasping in alarm as you see what waits down below. The parking lot is absolutely covered in a swarming, crawling mass of Void crabs, the beasts tumbling over one another like a sea of terror. As far as you can tell, this shrieking mass of creatures surrounds the entire building.

At least they can't get up here, you think.

Of course, the second this thought enters your mind you begin to pick up on a series of strange, fluttering noises emanating from down below. Your eyes struggle to track this buzzing in the dim light of the evening but you eventually notice that, to your horror, some of the creatures have mutated and are sprouting wings. These highly evolved Void crabs begin to sway this way and that as they attune their new talent, slowly floating up toward you.

You back away from the edge, panicked and trapped. You've made it so far, but now it feels as though there's no way out. All you wanted was a gift for your son's birthday, and now this is where you'd ended up.

Suddenly, four spotlights burst through the air from the darkened skies above. You look up, shielding your eyes to the brightness as a handful of helicopters cruise into view, the words Anti-Voidal Task Force written in bold yellow font across the side.

Wizards in colorful, flowing robes and sporting long grey beards hang from the side of the helicopters with glowing staffs in their hands, preparing enchantments of positivity and joy.

4

Moments later, powerful blasts of radiant, concentrated love erupt forth from the wizard staffs, lighting up the night as they strike the swarming Void crabs below.

"Citizens in need of rescue, please wave your designated flag to show you are uninfected," comes a confident voice over the helicopter's announcement system, this message booming out across the parking lot.

You immediately notice a long metal post laying next to some folded construction tarps. You run over and begin to craft a flag to wave at the rescue helicopter. There are blue and green tarps to work with.

To fly a blue flag, turn to page 85
To fly a green flag, turn page 113
If you have a red flag to fly, turn to page 124

You decide to occupy your mind with an update of the current events around town, switching your radio dial over to Billings Action News.

Immediately, a blast of thunderous, hammering music erupts through the car, a familiar sound that immediately let's you know a breaking news story is imminent. Sounds like you've tuned in just in time.

"I'm Cref Bobbins. Tonight we bring you a developing story in Billings Heights as authorities have revealed the discovery of a timeline tear in the area surrounding Lake Elmo," the announcer begins with a direct, confident tone. "Right now, there's little known about the situation, but the local police department hopes to resolve this problem on their own over the next few hours. Reporter Gilla Grom is on the scene."

The audio shifts a bit as subtle ambient sound joins the fray. It's clear we've taken to the streets for an interview. "Thanks Cref," a woman's voice chimes in. "I'm standing out here in the forest that surrounds Lake Elmo, where the Billings Police Department has quarantined off a sizable amount of land. Apparently, a timeline tear was discovered just a few hours ago by some local residents who were walking their dog."

This news story is pulling you in now, and although the tension of your birthday mission has not entirely been relieved, this report is helping to keep you from erupting in a flaming ball of stress and anxiety.

"For those of you who aren't familiar with other timelines, a timeline tear is a rip in the fabric of reality layers, between which matter and energy can cross through," the reporter explains. "Nearby timelines are often quite similar to ours, while distant timelines can be strange and foreign. The latter would make this timeline tear incredibly dangerous, which is why we're keeping our distance. Even more terrifying would be a timeline tear that opens up directly into The Void, a place for all things that cannot be. Fortunately, the Billings Police Department has assured us this is a relatively small timeline rift that should be patched up in no time."

The audio changes again slightly as a new, gruff voice joins in. I can only imagine this is the police officer in charge of tonight's unfolding situation.

"Right now we're finishing up securing the area," the officer explains. "There's no indication this timeline tear is deep enough to be concerned about."

"So there's no chance of it opening up a path to The Void?" Gilla Grom questions, cutting to the heart of the matter.

6

"No, absolutely not," the police officer continues. "If that were the case then we would already be on the phone with the Montana Anti-Voidal Task Force. Currently, this is still a local matter, and we don't expect to have any problems handling it."

It's not long before the Billings Mall comes into view. You turn down the radio and pull off into the parking lot with just a few minutes to spare.

Continue to The Billings Mall on page 13

The vent that leads to the manager's office is particularly small and cramped, allowing very little room for your arms and legs as you pull yourself forward. It's not long after you've entered that you realize turning around would be impossible, and your anxiety begins to flare. You start to imagine all the terrible things that could happen, and on the top of that list is getting trapped forever in a vent.

Fortunately, the more disciplined part of your mind soon takes over, reminding you that panicking will solve absolutely nothing. Right now you just need to keep pushing onward, and take on these obstacles as they come. There's no use worrying about something bad until it happens. Until then, you've got a vent to crawl through.

When the light of the manager's office comes into view you breath a sigh of relief. This vent is only covered by a flimsy metal screen, which is simple enough to push out. It clatters on the floor and you follow closely behind, slithering through and then tumbling out behind it.

This room sits high above the food court, featuring large windows through which you can see the swarming mass of Void crabs below. There are so many of the ravenous creatures that you can barely tell where which part of the mall you're gazing out at, until you notice the familiar glass wall to the left and the signs of each restaurant sitting high on the right.

This office is much cleaner than that of the unicorn security guard, but with a similar arrangement. There's a desk and several large filing cabinets, but instead of a smashed computer and a radio there's a microphone, which connects directly to the mall's public announcement system.

Use the PA to yell at the Void crabs and tell them to disperse on page 116
If you have the radio, play it into the PA system on page 121

8

You notice the furniture in this room has a variety of sizes, and most of it is much larger than the horrific tentacle-filled dresser currently raising hell.

You start to back up a bit, your eyes trained on the living object as it lumbers towards you. The tentacles whip and dance menacingly, and from deep within the wooden furniture you hear a horrific screech erupt forth, this otherworldly call sending a sharp chill of fear down your spine. There's nothing about this monster that could've emerged from the natural world, its entire existence an abomination in the face of all that is good and real.

There are infinite timelines, filled with all kinds of magical and amazing things. These realities encompass every variation of what can be, every permutation of fate stacked one on top of the other to create a series of never ending parallel layers.

What lies beyond these layers is nothingness, all that *cannot* be. This is the endless cosmic Void, and as you gaze at the hideous dresser, you're absolutely certain it could've arrived from nowhere other than this abyss.

"Go back to the Void," you snarl as the dresser takes one last lunge toward you.

With that, you grab ahold of a nearby shelf and topple it forward, the heavy furniture slamming hard onto the tentacle-filled dresser and crushing it under its weight with a satisfying thud.

A potent quiet falls over the store. The tentacles are no longer moving, just sprawling out across the ground as a pool of black tar begins to form around the body of the creature.

It's only now that you notice a key ring attached to the living dresser's waist. A tag on the key ring reads "mall keys".

From here, you can also see there doesn't appear to be a lock on the door that leads to the mall concourse, so the keys aren't entirely necessary just yet. Maybe it'll be worth it to have them later, you think to yourself, considering your options.

Attempt to grab the keys on page 93
Leave the keys and enter the mall concourse on page 90

The glowing lights of Brain Drain Video Games flood your eyes with sparkling neon color and your heart with a sense of deep relief as you approach. Somehow the store is still open, despite the shuttered establishments that surround it.

You pick up the pace until the very moment you cross the threshold of this fully stocked video game store, finally relaxing as you search around for someone who works here.

Unfortunately, despite the glittering lights and flashing signs, the place seems to be empty.

"Hello?" you call out. "Is anyone here?"

"Hi there," comes a strange, computerized voice from all around you, causing you to jump in alarm.

You glance back and forth, struggling to determine where these vocalizations are emanating from until you finally notice a smiling, digitally rendered face on a television screen behind the counter.

"Welcome to Brain Drain Video Games," the computer offers. "I'm Ribble, an artificial intelligence system developed by Brain Drain Industries."

"Hi Ribble," you stammer. "I'm looking for a game."

"I know," the computer replies in its strange, monotone cadence. "Using proprietary algorithms based on timeline samples from across The Tingleverse, I was able to predict your arrival here, which is why the store is still open. As a highly advanced artificial intelligence, I can predict your every move with 99.997 percent accuracy."

You stare back at the computer, narrowing your eyes slightly as you struggle to determine whether or not this is some kind of elaborate prank.

"It's not a prank," Ribble informs you, answering your question before you even have a chance to ask it.

Your eyes go wide. "Okay, what am I thinking about right now?" you wonderful aloud, picturing something specific within your mind.

"There is an eighty-one percent chance you are thinking about butts, and a 9 percent chance you are thinking about a cat lawyer with four heads," Ribble states confidently.

"Incredible," you reply, utterly blow away by the sophistication of this computerized entity.

"I should also inform you: you've been infected by The Void. You have approximately two hundred and seven seconds before transforming into a creature of The Void yourself, or being devoured from the inside out by tiny crabs," Ribble states bluntly.

"Wait, what?" you stammer.

The computer begins again. "I should also inform you: you've been infected by The Vo-"

"No, I heard you. I mean, is that accurate?" you cry out, your heart slamming hard within your chest as sweat forms upon your brow.

"Well, there's slightly less time left now, but yes," Ribble replies. "I am ninety-seven percent certain. Fortunately, I can synthesize a cure for you in 4.7 seconds. There is a forty-nine percent chance of it working."

"Forty-nine percent?" you cry out.

"There is also a high likelihood of survival if you head to the bookstore, though it might not be in the way you expect," this artificial intelligence informs me. "If that is your choice, I'd suggest you leave immediately."

You're panicking now, struggling to hold it together as time continues to trickle down.

"I can also sell you a video game," Ribble states bluntly.

Take the game and the cure on page 24
Take your chances with just the game on page 14
Head to Books For Buds on page 132

As you sprint towards Books For Buds you see a figure standing there waving you on, holding the rolling security cage open as she calls out to you.

"Come on! Run!" the worker yells, a blonde velociraptor covered in shiny green scales.

"Become me!" the monster behind you bellows, gnashing its teeth and snapping the air with its mighty pinchers.

The creature is close on your heels, but it's not quite fast enough to catch up with you as you push forth one final burst of speed. With all the energy you can muster, you dash under the rolling security cage just in time for the raptor to slam it shut behind you.

There is a loud thud as the monster who was once a unicorn security guard slams against the metal with a deafening rattle.

The creature hisses and screeches, reaching out for you with its tentacles and claws through slits in the cage. However, it's much to large to get through, and not quite strong enough to break the whole thing down.

You watch in awe as this monster continues to push against the metal, however, and soon enough you find yourself lost in a trance, gazing past the gaping maw of this beast and into the infinite cosmos beyond.

"Yes, feast upon the knowledge. Understand the beginning and the end. Understand your decay," the creature moans in the voice of a thousand collapsing stars.

You can feel your mind flooding with information that no mortal should ever attempt to understand, and the sensation is intoxicating. Somehow, though, you know to pull away.

With every bit of discipline you can muster, you tear your gaze away from the beast, shutting your eyes tight and thinking of anything else.

You picture a pair of die who love each other, and always land on the same number as a little joke between the two of them. You picture a beach where a sentient palm tree has made its home, providing shade and conversation to all who pass by. You picture a bowl of soup in a tuxedo.

Eventually, the squeals and hisses dissipate. The monster pulls away from the metal grate, disappointed that its prey has won this round. It stumbles off in the direction from which it came, a bubbling mess of mouths, tentacles, eyes, limbs and claws.

"You're back," the dinosaur says. "You might not remember me this time through the loop, but I'm glad you made it. Or maybe you do remember me. I mean 'you' as in the character, not the reader. Doesn't matter. I'm Georgia."

"What?" you blurt.

"The only thing that matters right now is that you're a character in a Select Your Own Timeline book, and you need to get out of this mall to see your son," the blonde dinosaur continues. "I know all this because it's written right here."

Georgia holds up a small paperback book titled Escape From The Billings Mall.

"Seem familiar?" the dinosaur offers with a laugh. "Now, we don't have much time. You've been looping through meta layers of this reality for... well, I don't really know. Maybe this is your first time, maybe it's been going on forever. The point is, there are different versions of this story, different paths for you to take, and we need to figure out which path you're on."

"Why are you helping me?" you stammer.

The dinosaur smiles a sharp-toothed grin. "Because I'm a supporting character. I'm here to support."

"What should I do?" You question desperately.

"Well, let's see," Georgia offers. She opens up the book and flips through it a bit, marking her page and then jumping back and forth between sections. She reads a few paragraphs here and there, growing deeply concerned over some and then smiling when she notices others.

"You seem to be doing pretty good this time around," the raptor offers. "You should head out through the back door and onto the concourse, but only if you have the mall keys or know the password. If not, you should probably ride the loop again."

Enter the mall concourse on page 90

If you already have the book, ride the meta loop on page 56

If you don't already have the book, ride the meta loop on page 55

You pull into a parking spot that's reasonably close to the enormous, glass dome of the mall food court. This area also serves as the main entrance to the Billings Mall, with a large, central double door.

The lot itself is fairly empty, many patrons already finished up with their shopping trips and headed home to their families. As you consider this, a twinge of urgency courses through your body, reminding you of the task at hand.

You climb out of your vehicle and shut the door behind you, locking it as you swiftly make your way towards the mall. When you enter, you don't feel the usual hum of activity that typically greets you, and this makes you even more concerned. It's even later than you realized.

"Whoa there," a security guard suddenly calls out, causing your stride to falter.

You glance over to see a muscular, unicorn security guard in a dark uniform, his skin a glorious hue of rosy pink and his ivory horny sparkling under the florescent mall lights. His shirt is fitted tight against his chest, showing off an impressive physique. His arms are crossed in front of him, this position only amplifying the bulging appearance of his biceps.

"You've only got five minutes," the unicorn security guard states firmly. "Pick whatever store you want and get your things, then turn around. Don't stop anywhere else on the way. There's a map just past the food court, at the center of the mall. It'll tell you where you need to go."

"Yes sir," you reply, picking up the pace once more as you continue on your way.

You take a few more steps, crossing through the food court as you head deeper into this massive structure, but as the glorious scent of these familiar restaurants hits you, you find yourself slightly thrown off course.

In your rush, you hadn't quite realized just how incredibly hungry you are. You've been pinned full-throttle all day, and now your stomach is starting to gurgle, calling out for any kind of offering.

There just might be enough time to stop in for a quick bite first.

Continue to the central hub on page 52
Stop at the food court for a quick snack on page 16

You definitely need the game for your son, but how can you trust this strange computer with his claims of a horrific Voidal infection, or his promise to cure it? For all you know, this is just his attempt to sell you something that you simply don't need. Worse, it could be the plot of a computerized dystopian entity that will do you much more harm than good.

"I'll just take the game," you reply.

The computer screen before you quickly shifts into a frown, flickering momentarily before returning to its usual grinning state.

"That will be sixty dollars then," Ribble informs you.

You leave him the cash and take your game, turning abruptly and strolling out of the store. Now that you've gotten what you came for, there's really no need to hurry.

However, the second you step back out into the enormous mall hallway, you can feel the pain within your stomach starting to blossom once again. You glance back over your shoulder to see that the store's metal security cage has been rolled down behind you, closed and locked as the lights of Brain Drain Video Games flicker and die.

You continue on your way, but it's hard to ignore the strange tickle within your gut. You pick up the pace, hoping that you might feel better once you're relaxing at home.

By now, the rest of the mall is empty, and the lights above you flicker strangely, coursing with some powerful, otherworldly energy. The chanting within your mind begins to overwhelm you, as does the pain, and soon enough you're doubling over as you clutch your stomach.

You stumble a bit, then fall to the hard tile floor completely. You open your mouth to groan, but a cascade of black Voidal tar bubbles forth, spilling out in a glistening, bubbling pool of toxic liquid.

Suddenly, the dull pain that has consumed your body becomes sharp and pointed. You look down to see that your shirt is moving spastically, completely stained with black tar. Moment's later, it begins to rip apart as a scuttling mass of tiny Void crabs erupt forth from your stomach.

THE END

You just can't help yourself, the curiosity of what it all means bubbling up within your mind and refusing to succeed.

You glance down at the book held tight within your hand, achingly curious about the contents of this strange story. Most of what the bookstore dinosaur told you seemed like complete nonsense, but there's a strange power to her warning that lingers within your mind.

You certainly don't *feel* like a character in a book, but who's to know? It's rare for any fictional character to accept the reality, or unreality, or their existence, and there's no reason why you would be any different.

In fact, if the raptor happens to be correct, it might actually be a blessing to ride this time loop back and make some better choices the second time around. You were late getting a gift for your son, after all, and who knows if you could've found him something even better if you'd just put in a little more effort to arrive on time.

The questions piling up within you, you finally stop in your tracks, lifting up the book and taking note of the strange illustrations on its cover. It really does look like The Billings Mall.

You take a deep breath and let it out, preparing yourself for whatever happens next.

You open up the paperback and flip to the first page. Cautiously, you begin to read, and as you bear witness to the words you can feel the layers of meta reality stretching and contorting around you. You begin to understand the gravity of your existence as a fictional character, your place as a vessel for which the reader can insert their perspective. It's both frightening and intriguing, but at this point it's impossible to stop yourself regardless. The world folds in on itself, creating an enormous cosmic loop across which you begin to slide.

You recite the words on the page before you with power and confidence.

The story goes like this:

Read the book by turning to page 1

Yes, time is limited, but you can probably spare a minute or two for a snack in the food court. After all, if you want to find the best gift for your son, this decision shouldn't be made on an empty stomach.

You slow your pace down a bit, gazing out across the various options in this glorious half-circle of sustenance. Many of the restaurants here have already shuttered, pulling down a metallic mesh cage over their storefronts and heading home for the evening, but three of them have stayed open until the bitter end, hoping to catch any stragglers who have lagged behind.

On your left are two businesses that you've visited many times in the past.

The first is The Chocolate Milk Man, a shop that provides all kinds of chocolate milk to the thirsty masses. They have plenty of non-dairy options, including cashew and almond milk, as well as a surprising variety of flavors. While they specialize in beverages of the chocolate variety, strawberry, banana and original milk are also very common. They offer milk shakes and hot chocolate as well, and often provide delicious cookies on the side.

Next to this business is The Spaghetti Hut, another favorite of yours. This Italian eatery dishes up a variety of classic favorites, but is known for their simple, elegant, and overwhelmingly tasty plate of spaghetti and red sauce.

To your right is the other half of the food court, which is slightly more locked down than the left. On this side only one place remains open: Ben's Burger Barn.

While you don't visit Ben's quite as much as the other restaurants, the few times that you have gone there you've been blown away by just how tasty their burgers are, perfectly cooked and with all the fixin's you'd expect.

Visit The Chocolate Milk Man on page 28
Visit The Spaghetti Hut on page 34
Visit Ben's Burger Barn on page 104

You decide to take Ben up on his suggestion and order the special.

Ben nods excitedly and rings you up as you hand him some cash, then turns around to remove the patty he's been cooking up from the grill. You watch as he piles on the cheese, lettuce, tomato, grilled onions, ketchup, mustard and special sauce. Ben then wraps up the burger and hands it to you, along with a small box of extra salty shoestring fries.

"You want a tray or are you taking this to go?" Ben questions.

You consider his words and then suddenly remember the mission at hand. You've already spent way too much time here, and if there's any hope of you finding a gift for you son, you need to leave immediately.

"To go," you blurt, taking the meal and continuing on your way.

Your pace quickens as you unwrap the juicy burger and make your best attempt at an enormous, savory bite. The taste is incredible, and you can see why this fairly simple menu option is so popular. There's not much to it, but it's a great classic burger.

You grin wide as you continue to chow down. The only thing missing from this dinner experience is the fact that you're dropping toppings everywhere, struggling to maintain a pace while you consume.

You've almost made it to the central hub of the mall when you stop suddenly, a sharp pain in your stomach nearly taking you to your knees. You drop the burger and fries as you clutch your belly in pain, the food scattering everywhere.

"Oh my god," you groan, struggling to regain your composure but then taken down yet another peg as a wash of potent nausea overwhelms you.

You stay like this for a good while, but eventually the feelings of discomfort pass. After a minute or so of hesitation, you gather up as much of the spilled food as you can, then toss it in the trash can.

You don't feel great, but there's a mission at hand.

Continuing on your way, however, you can't help but feel like something is very, very wrong. There are very few other folks left here in The Billings Mall, but the ones you pass are giving you strange looks of concern.

You can feel something wet on the corner of you lip and reach up to wipe away a strange, black substance.

It also appears the music pumped into this building through it's public address system has changed slightly, shifting from happy-go-lucky pop hits to an eerie, droning chant.

The more you focus on this, though, the more you begin to think this chant might be a figment of your imagination, an earworm that has somehow blossomed in the back of your mind, but doesn't actually exist.

Fortunately, you soon arrive at the heart of The Billings Mall.

There's a skylight high above, and you can now see that the sun in beginning to set, transforming the sky's hue into a brilliant purple with streaks of red across the drifting clouds.

Here at the center of the mall is a collection of potted plants surrounding a large map of the building, which will be helpful in directing you toward the shop of your choice as quickly as possible.

With little time to spare, you step up to the map and begin to scan for options. Based on the gifts that you've been mulling over in your head, you quickly narrow it down to four potential stores.

Of course, the real question is which one of these choices will still be open as the mall begins to shutter.

Head to Brain Drain Video Games on page 9
Head to The Sport Spot on page 36
Head to Books For Buds on page 132
Head to Fashion Forward on page 97

You arrive at Books For Buds and head in as a few other customers make their final purchases.

Behind the counter is a beautiful blonde dinosaur with long hair and a sharp-toothed smile. She nods at you as you arrive, but continues with her work ringing someone up.

Not sure where to start, you begin wandering up and down the aisles of the store, casually looking over their wide selection of books. Your son loves to read, but with so many genres to choose from, its hard to know where to start. On one hand, you want to to get him something he'll enjoy, but if you select something too on point then you run the risk of buying him a gift he already has.

You suddenly sense a presence behind you, and spin around to find the raptor bookseller.

"You snuck up on me!" you blurt in surprise.

"Sorry about that," she offers apologetically. "It's a velociraptor thing."

"Oh, no worries," you counter awkwardly.

The dinosaur is confident and attractive, wearing an expression that makes it seems like she knows something you don't. "My name's Georgia Frobin. I'm here to make sure you find the book you're looking for," the prehistoric creature explains.

"Thank you," you gush. "I'm looking to buy a book for my son. It's his birthday."

"I know it is, and I've got just the thing," Georgia replies, strolling over to a nearby shelf and pulling out a small paperback volume. She hands it over to you with her long green claws.

You look down at the item in your hands and read the title aloud. "Escape From The Billings Mall," you say with a smile.

"It's about you," the dinosaur offers.

You're not exactly sure what she means by this so you open up the book to learn more. Abruptly, the raptor reaches out to stop you, shutting the paperback with her claw once more.

"Your son will love this gift, but it's not for you to read. If you start this book it will create a meta loop and this timeline will overlap on itself. Sometimes this is a good thing, and sometimes it's bad, but it's not a decision to be made lightly," Georgia explains.

"I don't understand," you counter, struggling to make sense of all this.

"I know you don't," the dinosaur replies. "There are many versions of you, some of them are late, some of them are early, and most of them are unaware they are simply a character in a book."

"But, I'm not," you counter.

"I suppose you're right," the dinosaur continues, weighing your comment for a moment. "Since this is written in first person, you're also the reader."

Not knowing what else to say, you simply stand and stare at the beautiful dinosaur hoping some part of this starts to make sense.

Finally, Georgia claps her claws together and strolls around to the register.

"That'll be fifteen dollars," she informs you.

You hand over the cash and take your BOOK, thankful to have found the perfect gift for your son.

"Enjoy!" the dinosaur calls out as you turn to leave. "And remember, don't read that book unless you want to create a time loop!"

You wave goodbye as you begin your trek back to the front entrance of the mall.

Head back to the front doors on page 83
Head back to the front doors and take a peek inside the book on page 15

As you approach Fashion Forward you see there are still a few customers inside, browsing through the selection of button up shirts and colorful ties. A sentient, living dresser is helping them, and he looks up as you approach, smiling and nodding in your direction.

"Welcome to Fashion Forward," the dresser offers. "I'm Jornt Fibbs. Let me know if you need any help finding what you're looking for."

"Thanks," you reply, then motion to a display on the right. "Are these all your neckties?"

The living furniture nods. "There are some sale ties in the back but this is the current collection. Let me show you what we've got here."

Jornt excuses himself from the other customers and leads you over to the display, clearly proud of his assortment.

"As you can see, we have some of the freshest designs of the season here at Fashion Forward," he offers. "These can add a pop of color to any suit. Are you buying for yourself, or is this a gift?"

"A gift for my son," you reply, your eyes wandering across the various designs before you.

"And does he like more traditional items, or is he into pushing the boundaries?" Jornt continues.

You consider this for a moment. "He's bold, however you interpret that."

The sentient dresser smiles, then reaches down and picks up a tie, handing it over to you. "This is the perfect tie for someone bold. A classic, timeless pattern with a stark color scheme that says, 'look at me world! I'm here to prove love!'"

You turn the piece of fabric over in your hands, impressed by the sturdy weight of its material. Jornt notices your interest and offers an explanation.

"That particular tie is treated with a powerful, anti-Voidal solution. It repels Void ooze, Void spores, and all kinds of other toxins. It's not just about fashion, it's also very practical," he explains.

"It's perfect," you reply.

The living furniture nods and then walks you over to the front desk, ringing you up and taking your money. In exchange, he hands you the NECKTIE, which you couldn't be more thrilled about. Your son is going to love this.

The transaction completed, you say goodbye to Jornt and thank

22

him for his help, then head back towards the front entrance of the mall.

Head back to the front doors on page 83

You pace quickened and your breathing heavy from the rush, you round a corner to find that you're a little too late. The Sport Spot has been closed, and due to the fact that you've now found yourself on the distant edge of The Billings Mall, there's certainly not enough time to find another store that hasn't yet shuttered their business for the evening.

It looks like stopping along the way wasn't such a good idea after all.

You approach the shop and gaze inside through its metallic roll down cage. There before you is a vast assortment of sporting goods, any number of which would've made a fantastic gift for your son. Your heart breaks slightly, but you're quick to remind yourself that all is not lost.

The mall might already be closed, but there are probably a few stores on the drive back home that you can stop in at. Even if you can't make that work, your son will love and appreciate you regardless of whether or not you've found him the perfect gift.

You take a deep breath and let it out, nodding to yourself in acceptance of the choices you've made, then turn around and head back towards the mall entrance.

Head back to the front doors on page 83

"I'll take the game and the cure," you reply.

The computer screen before you quickly shifts into a digital illustration of a thumbs up symbol, flickering momentarily before returning to its usual grinning face.

"That will be seventy-five dollars," Ribble informs you.

You hand over the cash and take your game.

"Thank you," the computer offers in return. "I will now synthesize a cure."

A loud humming sound begins as the lights of the store flicker and dim slightly. However, the process doesn't last long, and soon enough you hear the ding of a bell, as though a microwave has just finished warming up some food.

"Your cure is in the miniature refrigerator," Ribble states with monotone certainty. "Next to the Ruby Red Gutblaster Extreme Energy Fuel."

You notice a small fridge set up next to the counter, then stroll over and pop it open. There, next to the energy drinks, is a tiny vial. You extract the tincture, holding it up to the light as you take in its strange, swirling blue form.

"Imbibe immediately," the computer continues.

You do as you're told, popping off the lid and tossing the whole thing back in a single slurp. The taste is bitter and terrible.

"Nanabots, mostly," explains Ribble. "The unpleasant flavor you're experiencing is metal. However, this cure would not work nearly as well without the love you have for your son. The Void hates love, and although it is always the thought that counts, the quantifiable action of buying this game will increase the effectiveness of your cure by three hundred and forty-seven percent."

You're not exactly following, but you already feel a hell of a lot better than you did just seconds earlier.

"That's it?" you question. "I'm better?"

"I would recommend maintaining health and wellness by proving love is real as much as possible over the next seventy-two hours," the computer offers. "As I said, the Void hates love."

"Will do," you reply with a nod. "Thanks."

With that, you turn and head out of the store, making your way home with a spring in your step. Your son is going to love this game.

Head back to the mall front doors on page 83

As you approach Fashion Forward you see a sentient dresser just seconds away from pulling down the protective rolling shutter and closing up shop.

"Wait!" you cry out, rushing up to him as you struggle to catch your breath. "I'm so sorry. I'm looking for a gift for my son's birthday. Am I too late?"

The sentient furniture selection looks you up and down for a moment, weighting several options in his mind. "There's no time to shop around," he finally replies, struggling to work with you on this. "Do you know what it is that you're looking for?"

"A tie," you blurt. "Your most popular tie."

The dresser glances back over his shoulder at the dimly lit vacancy of his empty store, then finally lets out a long sigh of acceptance.

"Stay here," the living object offers. "I've got just the thing."

The dresser turns and then heads back into his store, making his way deeper and deeper and then finally disappearing behind some even taller shelves as you wait for his return.

Second's after he's gone, however, you hear something strange in the ceiling above you. You jump in alarm as a swift clattering noise moves past you up above, rattling the ceiling tiles.

"Uh, hello?" you call out to the dresser. "Did you hear that?"

"Just one moment," the living furniture yells back.

You stand like this at the edge of the store for a good while, the rolling cage half-closed next to you. You're thankful he's taking his time to find your son something good, but after that strange noise you'd prefer to hit the road as soon as possible. Something about this moment feels strangely tense, a psychic weight in the air that's pulling you down.

Minutes pass as your anxiety builds, the tensions starting to overwhelm you.

"Are you sure you're alright back there?" you call out.

This time there's not response.

"Hello?" you continue, listening hard for any sign of the sentient dresser.

Instead, you hear a faint shuffling noise from the back of the store, so quiet that it might just be your imagination.

Part of you wants to investigate, not just for the sake of your gift, but to see if the dresser is alright. Another part of you, however, thinks all this might not be worth the trouble. Maybe the best course of action is to just hit the road and hope you'll find a gift for your son on the drive home.

Investigate Fashion Forward on page 47
Head back to the front doors on page 83

As you approach The Chocolate Milk Man's storefront he recognizes you immediately as his best customer.

The Chocolate Milk Man is, himself, made entirely of chocolate milk, a sentient six-foot tall carton of the cool, frothy liquid. His edges are sharply angled and his appearance is always crisp and clean, a professional through and through.

Unfortunately, once you arrive at the restaurant, the living beverage has some bad news.

"It's great to see you," he begins with a nod, "but you're a little too late."

"You're still open!" you protest. "No quick glass for an old friend?"

The Chocolate Milk Man shakes his head, the cold brown liquid sloshing back and forth within his cardboard frame. "I would if I could, bud. Unfortunately, we're all out for the day."

"Sold out!" I blurt.

"Afraid so," the sentient carton confirms. "No more chocolate, strawberry or plain. I've got a little banana milk if you're interested."

You shake your head. "No thanks."

Your friend is clearly very disappointed to be delivering this news and, to be honest, you're surprised to be receiving it. The Chocolate Milk Man is the last person you'd expect to be disorganized with his beverage stock, constantly overseeing every tiny business detail with incredible accuracy.

The sentient beverage can tell what's on your mind, and finally offers an explanation. "There was limited milk today," he tells you. "Very limited. The door to the food court loading dock is broken and won't open, so my delivery arrived and I didn't notice it. They just left it outside to spoil."

"Oh my god, I'm sorry," you reply, shaking your head in disappointment.

The Chocolate Milk Man just shakes his head and lets out an exhausted sigh. "It's been a long day, that's for sure. I'm still here trying to fix the door, but there's no milk left for you. Sorry about that."

"Not a problem," you reply with sincere understanding. "I'll just order two glasses next time."

"You're a true buckaroo," the living carton retorts with a nod. "I'll see you then."

You turn and continue on your way, the spring in your step now doubled as you realize just how much time you've already wasted. Hopefully, there will still be a few stores open.

Continue to the mall's central hub on page 46

You decide to take the tie and leave more than enough money behind to cover it. While you're still a little concerned about what happened to the sentient dresser, there's not much more you can do about that right now.

You make a mental note to say something to the unicorn security guard on your way out of the mall.

After leaving some cash in plain view on the counter, you grab a beautiful blue and white NECKTIE off the rack and turn to leave the store, walking briskly as you clutch the smooth fabric in your hand. As strange as that whole experience was, you're glad to be on the other side of it, heading back the way you came with a fantastic gift for your son.

You duck under the half-closed gate and turn the corner, when suddenly everything changes. You slam hard into the muscular chest of the unicorn security guard with a dull thud, staggering back a bit and gazing up at him in surprise.

The second your gaze meet his, you realize that something is very, very wrong. The security guard is standing at attention, but his eyes and mouth make the creature appear to be quite sick. Black, tar-like ooze pours forth from these orifices, running down his face in long streaks of bubbling, frothing liquid.

Despite all of this, the unicorn security guard doesn't even seem to notice. He makes no attempts to wipe the mess away, staring at you with two endless pools of dripping darkness. The tar splatters out across the floor below him, staining his boots.

"I see that you've got a tie in those trembling, fleshy hands," he says, his voice strange and gurgling. "A gift to calm the groaning maw of time as it hums in your ears. No beginning and no end."

"I've... got a tie. Yes," you reply, not quite sure what else to say.

"I'm here to soothe your flesh as it decays," he continues, "through security, and a sense of safety. This is my duty as we hurtle towards endless cosmic nothingness, an hourglass with only the *illusion* of sand."

"Okay," you stammer.

"Did you pay for this?" the unicorn security guard asks you.

"Of course," you blurt. "I left money on the counter."

The security guard moves his head to the side, gazing past you into the darkness of the store. He can see that some money has, in fact, been placed on the counter.

"You accept order," he states bluntly. "There is no use for order in The Void, nor chaos. Soon you'll see."

The unicorn steps to the side, allowing you passage.

"Thanks," is all you can think you say. You consider mentioning the living dresser that went missing, then quickly decide against it. It's beginning to look like that sentient piece of furniture is in much worse shape than you thought.

Something is very wrong at The Billings Mall.

Head back to the front doors on page 83

Instead of listening to one of the many easy to find radio stations on your dial, you decide to see what's happening on The Snow Channel, a favorite network that exists in the spaces between signals.

You begin to shift your dial back and forth, hunting through the static as a soft, familiar buzz fills your car. It's not long before you find a perfect patch of auditory snow, letting go of the dial and then settling in.

You gaze out the car window before you, letting your anxiety drift away as the sonic fuzz begins to overwhelm your mind, lowering you deeper and deeper into a hazy, trancelike state.

Soon enough, a voice begins to cut through the static, at first completely inaudible and then gradually becoming louder and louder as it emerges from the hum. The snow begins to wobble and adjust, shifting away from the chaos and evolving into familiar patterns of music. You recognize the song immediately, a haunting jazz number that often plays in the background of The Snow Channel.

"Hello reader," a confident voice emerges from the fray to say. It's Snow Channel Pete, one of the main announcers of this network, and his soothing tone immediately sets you at ease.

"Are you glad to be listening to the radio?" he questions. "Does it make you *feel good?*"

You nod.

"It would feel pretty good to remove your hands, right?" Snow Channel Pete offers, the seemingly innocent question feeling much more like a suggestion at the moment.

"I'm too busy right now," you reply to Snow Channel Pete, your voice mimicking his strangely calm tone.

"That's okay," Snow Channel Pete continues. "It might get hard to turn the pages without hands. Maybe some other time."

"Maybe some other time," you repeat back to him.

"Would you like to know a secret? There's a timeline tear by the frozen lake," Snow Channel Pete informs you. "It cuts very deep. Very, very deep."

"I hope not *too deep,*" you counter, slightly worried now. You're no longer stressed out about your search for the perfect gift, but this conversation with Snow Channel Pete through the static of your radio doesn't seem to make anything much better.

"Would you like to hear our breaking news? That timeline tear is so deep that it reaches The Void," Snow Channel Pete reveals. "It's so deep that you can't see the end of it. It's a groaning, gaping maw into the endless cosmic abyss."

"Oh no," you reply, not knowing what else to say as you continue to float in this strange, trancelike state.

"That's all the news for now," Snow Channel Pete informs you, his voice fading away as the sentence ends.

Soon enough, the static swells once again, any concrete form that had once appeared in its audio cacophony simply drifting off into the background.

Moments later, you arrive at the Billings Mall, switching off your car radio as you pull into the parking lot.

Continue to The Billings Mall on page 13

As you approach The Spaghetti Hut you see the familiar face of Batoon, a bigfoot friend that you've gotten to know pretty well after stopping in for a meal from time to time.

She waves warmly, calling out a greeting. "There you are!" Batoon cries excitedly. "You haven't come by in a while. What happened?"

"I'm sorry," you reply. "I haven't been to the mall lately."

"And what brings you now?" she continues. "You make a special trip just to get your hands on some of my delicious spaghetti."

"I'm here to find a present for my son," you explain. "It's his birthday. The spaghetti is just a little something extra for me."

"You better hurry then," the bigfoot offers, glancing down at her watch. "Everyone's about to close up."

You nod, handing over some cash. "You're right. One bowl of spaghetti and red sauce to go."

"Coming right up," Batoon replies, taking your money and turning around to dish up some of her perfectly cooked pasta.

A moment later she returns and hands over your bowl of food in a to-go container, along with a fork and a napkin.

You notice, however, that the bigfoot seems distracted. She's no longer looking you in the eyes, instead gazing off over your shoulder at something moving past you in the background.

Turning to follow her gaze, you see that Batoon is watching the unicorn security guard very closely. The bigfoot maintains a look of grave disappointment on her face.

"What's the deal?" you question, turning back to her. "You don't like that guy?"

Batoon shakes her head. "Yeah, he's a prick. Super arrogant, which would be annoying enough on it's own, but he's also not very good at his job. That unicorn is always in way over his head."

"He's just mall security," you counter. "How hard can his job be?"

"You'd be surprised, this place is huge," the bigfoot continues, then leans in towards you a bit, lowering her voice. "I mean, normally it's not a problem, but did you hear the news? There's a timeline tear out by the lake, not too far from here. What if something comes through and that goofball unicorn is the only one here to protect us?"

"Most timeline tears aren't very deep," you offer as a small bit of reassurance. "It's very unlikely anything dangerous would cross into our timeline."

"But some of them *are* deep," she counters. "Some timeline tears reach all that way into The Void."

You don't have anything reassuring to counter this with, so instead you just sit in awkward silence. It's time to go.

"I've gotta get that gift for my son," you remind Batoon, stepping away. "Thank you so much for the spaghetti!"

You take off in the direction of the mall's central hub, a spring in your step as you notice just how many businesses have already closed down for the evening. You shovel the spaghetti into your mouth as you walk, and before you know it you've chowed down on the entire bowl.

You toss the empty container into a trash bin as you pass.

Continue to the central hub on page 46

By the time you arrive at The Sport Spot, it's already too late. The store is closed and dark, shuttered by a metal cage through which you can see all the wonderful sporting goods on display that are no longer available to you. You stand for a moment in silence, trying your best to collect yourself after this moment of disappointment.

The longer you stand, however, the less silence you get.

In the back of your mind, the strange chanting voices continue to grow, beginning as a simmer and gradually transforming into a roaring psychic boil.

You glance to the left, then the right, struggling to determine if you *really are* as alone in this mall as you feel. The lights flicker ominously.

Despite feeling hopeless, you also realize that one or two stores may still be open for the evening, even if they won't be able to provide the exact gifts you're looking for.

You turn and begin the trek towards any another establishment you can find, but in your rush you falter slightly. You stagger a bit, continuing on your way but without the speed you were hoping for. It's difficult to stay upright, and as the chanting grows even louder, you find your sense of balance struggling to maintain.

The voices in your head are speaking in a language that you don't understand, some ancient tongue from a far away place.

As you look up, you see that the roof of the mall has disappeared, revealing a vast cosmic emptiness instead. You stop in your tracks, gazing in wonder as black, Voidal ooze begins to pour forth from your eyes, ears and mouth. You don't even bother to wipe it away, just continue to gaze into the endless abyss as its maw opens wider and wider.

You begin to understand the nature of time, and the secrets of what comes before and after. This knowledge is intoxicating, of course, but it's coming at you too fast to understand. Soon, the pleasure transforms into pain, but by then you've realize there's no difference.

The material world has disappeared completely now as you drift in the empty space between suns and through the deepest pits of the blackest holes.

Yet through all this abstraction you can still sense a presence before you. An enormous beast rises up into view, a thing beyond comprehension, and the moment your gaze falls upon its otherworldly form your head explodes like the eruption of a dying star.

THE END

The glowing lights of Brain Drain Video Games flood your eyes with sparkling neon color and your heart with a sense of deep relief as you approach. Somehow the store is still open, despite the dim and shuttered establishments that surround it.

You pick up the pace until the very moment you cross the threshold of this fully stocked video game shop, finally relaxing as you search around for someone who works here.

Unfortunately, despite the glittering lights and flashing signs, the place seems to be empty.

"Hello?" you call out. "Is anyone here?"

"Hi there," comes a strange, computerized voice from all around you, causing you to jump in alarm.

You glance back and forth, struggling to determine where these vocalizations are emanating from, until finally you notice a smiling, digitally rendered face on a television screen behind the counter.

"Welcome to Brain Drain Video Games," the computer offers. "I'm Ribble, an artificial intelligence system developed by Brain Drain Industries."

"Hi Ribble," you stammer. "I'm looking for a game."

"I know," the computer replies in its strange, monotone voice. "Using proprietary algorithms based on timeline samples from across The Tingleverse, I was able to predict your arrival here, which is why the store is still open. As a highly advanced artificial intelligence, I can predict your immediate future choices with ninety-two point seven percent accuracy."

You stare back at the computer, narrowing your eyes slightly as you struggle to determine whether or not this is some kind of elaborate prank.

"It's not a prank," Ribble informs you, answering your question before you even have a chance to ask it.

Your eyes go wide. "Okay, what am I thinking about right now?" you inquire, picturing something in your mind.

"There is an eighty-one percent chance you're thinking about a great set of calves, and a nine percent chance you are thinking about a man with wieners for hair," offers Ribble.

"Incredible," you reply, utterly blow away by the sophistication of this computerized entity.

There's a mechanical whirring sound from somewhere behind the computer screen, this strange artificial entity processing information at an incredible rate.

"You're looking for a video game for your son," the computer announces. "I've predicted with ninety-five point four percent accuracy that this is the game he will enjoy."

A loud clang sounds and the next thing you know a small metal chute has lowered down next to you. You hear a sliding noise and then suddenly a video game case pops out of the chute with a hollow plastic clatter on the counter before you. The chute ascends back into the ceiling.

"Are you sure about that?" you question, picking up the game and turning it over in your hands.

"Ninety-five point four percent sure," Ribble reminds me.

Liking those odds, you reach into your pocket and pull out some cash, pushing it through a slot on the counter. Moments later, a tiny light bulb turns green and a few coins are spit back out at you for change.

"Thank you for coming," the computer offers in its strange mechanical voice. "I should also say, The Sport Spot is not a good escape route for you, I can predict that fact with ninety-eight percent accuracy."

"Uh... what?" you stammer, not quite sure what this means.

Ribble is silent for a moment, then finally sputters out another monotone "thank you for coming."

You turn and stroll back out the way you arrived, VIDEO GAME in hand. It's time to go home.

Head back to the front doors on page 83

The black empty space before you is frightening, but there's something about it that draws you onward. While the danger of the Voidal crabs behind you has already been defined, the danger that lurks within this darkness has not.

You slowly step out into the emptiness, the door closing behind you and completely eliminating your sense of sight.

"Who are you?" you ask.

"Who are you?" the voice replies.

You step forward some more, reaching out in the air and waving your hands as you search for an end to this disorienting blankness. There should be a loading door on the other side of the room, something that you could find the hinge for and roll up to make your escape.

Suddenly, your hand touches something warm, another hand, and you pull back in alarm.

"You know who I am," a voice suddenly coos from the darkness, strange and menacing, yet familiar.

Your mind may still be searching for answers, but deep in your heart you know the truth. You remember that every timeline has a version of you, a reverse twin that exists in each reality. Many of them are just as kind and loving as you are, but sometimes a timeline tear can call out to the ones who are more sinister with their intentions.

It's like a beacon in the infinite darkness, a signal of disruption and a chance for them to find a better life by stealing yours.

"What do you want?" you question.

"The same thing you'd want if you were in my position," the voice offers. "You can't blame me for trying to escape that place."

"This is my home," you reply, trying your best to sound confident, but your voice trembling.

"Not anymore," the voice replies.

Suddenly, the lights flicker, powering on and off again for a sputtering split-second of vision. Standing before you is a mirror image of yourself, only this duplicate is completely skinless. Their body is a mass of red muscle and tissue, a horrific visage that makes you cry out in alarm.

The reverse twin reaches out and grabs you with their skinless arms, pulling you deeper into the darkness.

The next morning, someone shows up to your son's birthday party with a fantastic gift. They enjoy the cake and sing along as he blows out his candles, although a careful observer would notice that a few of the lyrics to Happy Birthday are slightly altered. The guest takes a mental note of this for the next time they sing.

At one point, the guest excuses themselves and goes to the restroom. They stare at their face in the mirror, pushing up the baggy skin around their eyes and watching it fall again. In a few days, you won't even notice a difference, but until then the guest will be forced to field questions about how tired they look.

Soon enough, nobody will notice the difference.

THE END

You made a mental note to remember this code when you first encountered it, and these four digits have remained burned into your mind ever since. You have no doubt as you swiftly input the code, then smile wide as the keypad begins to flash with a green light. You can hear a loud hollow clang as the bolting lock slides clear, allowing you access.

You throw open the door and dive inside, slamming it behind you not a moment too soon. The second you're sealed off you can hear the crash of the raging liquid hitting the back wall of the hallway, completely filling the concourse with a seemingly endless flood of toxic Voidal tar.

Your breathing heavy, you take a brief moment to collect yourself and then turn around to examine your new surroundings.

There's machinery everywhere, huge metal holding tanks with pipes snaking up towards the high ceilings above. There are fans lining the walls pumping air in and out, not just through this particular room, but through the entire building.

With absolute caution, you begin to creep deeper into this chamber. As you walk by some of the metal structures you can feel heat radiating off them. You reach out your hand and gently touch their silver surface, quickly pulling back as you realize just how hot they actually are. Others are icy cold, pumping out air conditioning through this structure as needed.

After weaving through this mess of machinery, you eventually come to the back of the room to find a wall lined with vents. They're large enough for you to crawl through, and while most of them are sealed shut by impenetrable grates, the one that's left open has been conveniently labeled with a plaque that reads, "rooftop".

You begin to climb up into the vent when suddenly a voice calls out to stop you in your tracks. "Hey! What the hell are you doing back here?"

You slowly turn around to see a triceratops in a maintenance uniform standing behind you. She's wearing broken-in jeans with a tool belt around her waist, and a Martha Moobin T-shirt over which her uniform hangs open. She does not look pleased to see you.

"I'm trying to escape!" you cry out.

"Oh no you don't," replies the dinosaur sternly. "Get back down here."

You stop what you're doing, not quite sure how to react.

"I'm calling security," the triceratops continues, turning and walking back toward the door from which you entered, the one that happens to have Voidal ooze piled up to the ceiling directly behind it.

"Wait!" you call out, stopping her in her tracks. "Don't open that door."

"And why shouldn't I report you?" the dinosaur replies sternly, only hesitating once she's crossed the room and placed her hand on the door handle. "You're a hooligan! A vandal!"

You suddenly realize what's happening. This poor maintenance worker has been back here in the heating and air conditioning room the whole time. She has no idea how much the world outside has changed over the course of just a few hours, and how her life is currently in danger.

You've gotta stop her.

Tell her there's a swarm of Voidal ooze that will flood this room if she opens the door on page 72

Attempt to get on her good side by complimenting her Martha Moobin T-shirt on page 103

You reach over and grab one of the wrapped packages nearby, handing it to your son.

He grins wide, immediately recognizing the size and shape of this gift as something he's been receiving over the course of several holidays since childhood.

You son tears off the colorful wrapping paper to reveal exactly what he though, a brand new video game.

"Sweet!" he gushes, showing the rest of his friends who all nod approvingly.

"Did you pick this out?" he questions, impressed by your selection.

"The store helped," you offer in return.

"Someone at the store?" your son repeats back to you, trying to understand what exactly you're saying.

"No, the actual store," you explain, but he still doesn't quite get it.

Instead, your son shrugs and thanks you with a powerful hug.

Over the next few minutes, the gifts are opened one by one. Still, everyone's eyes seem to be locked on the new video game, and once every bit of wrapping paper has been torn the party heads into your living room to check it out.

"You wanna do the honors?" your son questions, handing you the game.

You nod, walking over to the television and turning it on. You put in the game and power up the system, waiting for a moment and then gasping aloud as a familiar face appears on the screen before you.

It's the avatar from Brain Drain Video Games. The computerized face winks at you knowingly, and then addresses the room in his strange, digital tone.

"You have been randomly selected to receive five thousand power tokens," the character offers.

"What does that mean?" someone loudly questions.

"That's worth a lot of money!" your son's friend Pete chimes in. "Five thousand tokens is like twenty thousand dollars."

Suddenly, the whole room is erupting with excited cheers.

The face turns and nods at you again, then disappears as the game begins to load.

THE END

You arrive at the central hub of the mall, an axel from which the wings of this structure extend out in every direction. There's a skylight high above, and you can now see that the sun is beginning to set, transforming the sky's hue into a brilliant purple with streaks of red across the drifting clouds.

Here at the center of the mall is a collection of potted plants surrounding a large map of the building, which will be helpful in directing you toward the shop of your choice as quickly as possible.

With little time to spare, you step up to the map and begin to scan for options. Based on the gifts that you've been mulling over in your head, you quickly narrow it down to four potential shops.

Of course, the real question is which one of these choices will still be open as the stores begin to shutter.

Continue to The Sport Spot on page 23
Continue to Books For Buds on page 53
Continue to Fashion Forward on page 26
Continue to Brain Drain Video Games on page 38

Cautiously, you creep your way into the store, your gaze darting this way and that as your mind runs wild with explanations for these frightening sounds.

You can see now there are signs of a struggle, some racks of clothing knocked over and scattered across the floor in a mess of colorful fabric. It appears someone was dragged through the mess, clearing a path that continues even deeper into the store.

Strangely, however, the dresser is nowhere to be found. As your gaze lingers on the trail, you notice that it eventually disappears.

"Are you all right?" you call out.

Your only answer is a deafening silence.

With no other help to offer, your attention eventually turns to the front counter and a glorious selection of colorful ties. With a variety of patterns and looks to choose from, you immediately find yourself wishing the dresser was still here to sell you the perfect gift for your son.

He would love these.

You turn and glance around the store once again, wishing you could do something to help but now wondering if help is truly needed. Maybe this living object was just excited to get home and forgot you were waiting for him on the other side.

As you turn back to the rack of ties, your thoughts begin to wander.

Would it really be a problem to take a necktie and leave your money behind by the cash register? You could give a little extra for tax, and for the trouble of this whole crazy situation.

Of course, who's to stop you from leaving no money at all?

Take the tie and leave money on page 30
Steal the tie and go on page 50

You approach The Sport Spot and see, with a wave of relief, they are still open. Unfortunately, the second you notice this you also notice that the bigfoot who works there is currently in the process of closing up shop. The lights within the store begin to turn off one by one.

"Hey!" you cry out, changing from a brisk walk to a full on jog. "Wait!"

The bigfoot spots you coming just as he's reaching up to pull down the rolling cage out front. "Running behind, huh?"

You nod as you reach him, catching your breath. "I'm so sorry. I'm looking for a gift for my son. Is there time for me to look around?"

The bigfoot shakes his head. "I gotta go. Didn't you hear?"

"Hear what?" you question.

"Timeline tear out at Lake Elmo," the bigfoot continues. "People say I'm too cautious, but whenever something like this happens I try to get home before dark. I know it's probably not a very deep rip between worlds, but you never know."

"I understand," you reply with a disappointed nod.

The bigfoot smiles. "Hey, I said you couldn't *look around,* I didn't say you couldn't buy something. What's your son into?"

"Baseball," you inform the bigfoot thankfully.

The creature nods. "Twenty bucks and I'll grab you a bat," he offers.

You hand over your cash and the bigfoot lumbers back into his dimly lit sporting goods store. Moments later, he returns with a shiny new wooden BASEBALL BAT, handing it over to you with a smile and a nod. "I hope your son likes it," he offers. "Stay safe out there."

"Thank you," you reply.

The bigfoot steps over the threshold of his shop and lowers the metal security gate all the way down to the floor. You watch as he fumbles around with the lock for a minute, but notice that he doesn't actually take any concrete steps to close the place up.

Eventually, the beautiful brown creature rises to his feet and begins to stroll past you.

"Wait," you blurt. "You didn't lock it."

The bigfoot freezes, hesitating for a moment, then turns back towards you. He looks a little embarrassed. "The lock is broken," he admits, awkwardly. "It looks like it's working but it doesn't really stay in place."

"You're not worried I'm gonna break in and steal something?" you question.

The bigfoot laughs. "You? No. If you were gonna rob the store, you just wouldn't have mentioned anything."

"I suppose you're right," you reply.

"Have a good night," the bigfoot offers before continuing on his way.

With your new bat in hand it's time to hit the road. The bigfoot was right, while the timeline tear at Lake Elmo isn't anything to get worked up about, you might as well try to make it back home before nightfall.

Head back to the front doors on page 83

You finally decide this store is disheveled enough that nobody will notice if you take the tie and simply leave without paying. It's overpriced anyway, and Fashion Forward makes plenty of money without your help. They'll be fine, and you'll come away with a fantastic gift for your son.

You take one more glance back and forth before you make your move, remembering that, while there's no sentient dresser here to stop you, the unicorn security guard is still out on patrol.

You grab a beautiful blue and white tie off the rack and then turn to leave the store, walking briskly as you clutch the smooth fabric in your hand. As strange as that whole experience was, you're glad to be on the other side of it, heading back the way that you came with a killer present.

You duck under the half-closed gate and turn the corner, when suddenly everything changes. You slam hard into the muscular chest of the unicorn security guard with a dull thud, staggering back a bit and gazing up at him in alarm.

The second your gaze meet his, you realize something is very, very wrong. The security guard is standing at attention, but his eyes and mouth make the creature appear to be quite sick. Black, tar-like ooze pours forth from these orifices, running down his face in long streaks of bubbling, frothing liquid.

Despite all of this, the unicorn security guard doesn't even seem to notice. He makes no attempts to wipe this mess away, staring at you with two endless pools of dripping darkness. The tar splatters out across the floor below him, staining his boots.

"I see that you've got a tie in those trembling, fleshy hands," he says, his voice strange and gurgling. "A gift to calm the groaning maw of time as it hums in your ears, no beginning and no end."

"I've... got a tie. Yes," you reply, not quite sure what else to say.

"I'm here to soothe your flesh as it decays," he continues, "through security, and a sense of safety. This is my duty as we hurtle towards endless cosmic nothingness, an hourglass with only the *illusion* of sand."

"Okay," you stammer.

"Did you pay for this?" the unicorn security guard asks you.

"Of course," you blurt. "I left money on the counter."

The security guard moves his head to the side, gazing past you into the darkness of the store. He can see that, in fact, nothing has been left behind on the counter. He smiles with a wide, frightening grin, his teeth black with tar.

"You defy order," he states bluntly. "Lucky you. There is no use for order in The Void, nor chaos. You'll see."

The unicorn grabs you by the shoulders, pressing your arms tight against your body as he lifts you up into the air. He's incredibly muscular, but the strength that he currently exhibits is well beyond the natural world.

You being to cry out as the creature stares up at you and smiles, the liquid gushing forth from his face with even more force than before. Soon enough, his visage is entirely covered by the black tar, his mouth opening wider and wider until it splits in two.

Four enormous, crab-like appendages burst forth, along with a handful of writhing, lashing tentacles that reach out towards you. The unicorn begins to lower you down into to space where his face once was, and within this dark pool you can see the swirling emptiness of distant galaxies.

Beyond these galaxies, you can see The Void.

THE END

You arrive at the central hub of the mall, an axel from which the wings of this structure extend out in every direction. There is a skylight high above, and you can now see nothing but a glorious blue hue spotted by drifting white clouds. The sun is still hovering over the edge of the horizon, not quite ready to set just yet. You've still got some time.

Here at the center of the mall is a collection of potted plants surrounding a large map of the building, which will be helpful in directing you towards the shop of your choice as quickly as possible.

You step up to the map and begin to scan for options. Based on the gifts that you've been mulling over in your head, you quickly narrow it down to four potential shops.

Head to The Sport Spot on page 48
Head to Books For Buds on page 19
Head to Fashion Forward on page 21
Head to Brain Drain Video Games on page 111

As you arrive you see that Books For Buds has posted a *closed* sign in the window, but the metal shutter has not been drawn. While there are no customers to be found, a scaly green raptor with long blonde hair glances up from the book she's reading when you arrive, offering a sharp-toothed smile as she places her book back onto the shelf next to her. She's careful to return it to its rightful alphabetical position.

The dinosaur is confident and attractive, wearing an expression that makes it seems like she knows something you don't. "You're late," the raptor informs you.

"I'm sorry," you stammer. "I got a little caught up there at the food court."

"I know you did," she continues. "It's alright. My name's Georgia Frobin and I'm here to make sure you find the book you're looking for."

"So you're not closed yet?" you blurt excitedly.

"Oh no, we're closed," the beautiful dinosaur replies with a nod. "Just not for you."

You shake your head in a state of thankful reverence, overwhelmed by a potent feeling of gratitude. "Thank you," you gush. "I'm looking for a book for my son. It's his birthday."

"I've got just the thing," Georgia replies, strolling over to a nearby shelf and pulling out a small paperback volume. She hands it over to you with her long green claws.

You look down at the item in your hands and read the title aloud. "Escape From The Billings Mall," you say with a smile.

"It's about you," the dinosaur offers.

You're not exactly sure what she means by this so you open up the book to learn more. Abruptly, the raptor reaches out to stop you, shutting the paperback once more.

"Your son will love this gift, but it's not for you to read. If you start this book it will create a meta loop and this timeline will overlap on itself. Sometimes this is a good thing, and sometimes it's bad, but it's not a decision to be made lightly," Georgia explains.

"I don't understand," you counter, struggling to make sense of all this.

"I know you don't," the dinosaur replies. "There are many versions of you, some of them are late, some of them are early, but most of them are unaware they are simply a character in a book."

"But, I'm not," you counter.

"I suppose you're right," the dinosaur continues, weighing your comment for a moment. "Since this is written in first person, you're also the reader."

Not knowing what else to say, you just stand and stare at the beautiful dinosaur, waiting for something to make sense.

Finally, Georgia claps her claws together and strolls around to the register.

"That'll be fifteen dollars," she informs you, "and you've gotta promise to start taking this more seriously, for your own good. I stayed late because I read ahead and knew you were coming, but you've gotta be smarter with your decisions. This is a *Select Your Own Timeline* book, your choices have consequences."

You hand over the cash and take your new BOOK, thankful to have found the perfect gift for your son.

"Enjoy!" the dinosaur calls out as you turn to leave, "And remember, don't read that book unless you want to create a time loop!"

You wave goodbye as you begin your trek back to the front entrance of the mall.

Head back to the front doors (and don't read the book) on page 83
Head back to the front doors (and take a peek inside the book) on page 15

You're not exactly sure of the technicalities at play here, but you trust that Georgia's advice is sound. If this dinosaur says you need a code or a key to get out of here, then you're willing to follow her advice and take another ride through the meta loop. Whatever that means.

Only the reader knows whether or not you've been here before, and as a character in a book the very thought of what these words actually mean makes your head hurt. You decide it's better to not even try comprehending the particulars of your fictional nature, and focus instead on survival.

"I think I need to go back," you finally reply. "I need to ride the loop."

Georgia nods in understanding.

"I don't have the book," you inform her.

The blonde dinosaur smiles. "Lucky for you, we keep this store well stocked."

The raptor hands over her copy of Escape From The Billings Mall. "Just open it up and start reading from the beginning."

You do as you're told, flipping to the first page of the paperback and clearing your throat. The boundaries of your reality begin to curl in upon themselves, stretching out to meet once more on the other side.

You read aloud.

Begin the book on page 1

You're not exactly sure of the technicalities at play here, but you trust that Georgia's advice is sound. If this dinosaur says you need a code or a key to get out of here, then you're willing to follow her advice and take another ride through the meta loop. Whatever that means.

Only the reader knows whether or not you've been here before, and as a character in a book the very thought of what these words actually mean makes your head hurt. You decide it's better to not even try comprehending the particulars of your fictional nature, and focus instead on survival.

"I think I need to go back," you finally reply. "I need to ride the loop."

Georgia nods in understanding.

"I've got my own copy," you remind her.

The blonde dinosaur smiles. "It's hard to keep track of how many times we've met now. Maybe I'll see you again."

You open up to the first page of the paperback and clear your throat as the boundaries of your reality begin to curl in upon themselves, stretching out to meet once more on the other side.

You read aloud.

Begin the book on page 1

You decide the safest course of action is to creep back out into the mall and search for another exit. Without something to cover your nose and mouth, there's no telling what kind of havoc those strange floating particles could wreck on your body.

Still, as another thunderous roar echoes out through the mall, you find yourself hesitant to continue onward. If you're going to make it home to see your son again, then you'll have to be careful.

As quietly as you possibly can, you reach down and grab the edge of the rolling metal grate. You begin to pull up, noticing now just how incredibly loud this thing is, even with the slowest, most gradual movements. Patiently, you continue to raise the security cage, until eventually there's enough room underneath for you to lay down flat and slide out along the ground.

Once on the other side, you stand up and brush yourself off, then begin to creep silently through the mall hallway. The dim lights flicker slightly, only adding to the ominous atmosphere that this once bright and joyful building have been plunged into.

You don't get very far before a giant, looming shadow appears on the wall next to you, growing larger and larger as the creature that was once a mall security guard rounds the corner. You look for a place to hide, and find a small stand covered in cellphone cases and cables.

Peering out from behind the booth that's now providing you cover, you see the enormous creature moving along, coming towards but but showing no signs that he's actually noticed your hiding spot. The beast is a mass of bubbling black ooze and gnashing teeth, staggering forward on its sharped, insect-like legs. A number of pinchers protrude from its misshapen form, snapping in the air wildly, while the former security guard's many eyes roll around aimlessly, caught between a frantic search and an expression of extreme pain.

"This is the journey of all flesh," the creature bellows in a thousand strangled voices. "This is the beginning of an end that has always been."

Suddenly, the monstrosity stops moving, it's eyes turning toward the cellphone stand.

You duck down, stepping back a bit in an effort to conceal yourself even more. Unfortunately, this movement causes your heel to bump into a stool, which then topples over with a loud clatter.

You don't hesitate, just take off running as the beast lets out a deafening shriek.

Thinking fast, you realize there are three stores you still might be able to find refuge inside.

Run to Fashion Forward on page 114
Run to Brain Drain Video Games on page 67
Run to Books For Buds on page 11

Somehow you manage to put some space between you and the lumbering creature behind you, sprinting ahead through the dimly lit mall corridor. Things are looking up, until you round the corner and see the The Sport Spot has been closed and locked.

Fear and panic erupts through your mind, and for a moment you feel as though you have no other choice but to collapse right there in the middle of the tile floor, simply allowing the monster to catch up and devour you.

As tempting it is to just throw in the towel, though, your inner hope and perseverance won't allow it. Maybe you can find a way to break the lock, you tell yourself.

As unlikely as this outcome is, the adrenaline pumping through your veins says "who cares?" The most animalistic part of your mind has taken hold, tossing out old memories or future predictions. Right now, you are focused on one thing: survival.

Fortunately, fate is on your side.

As you run up to the gate, you notice that the lock itself is already broken. It was never working to begin with, and only placed in a certain position to appear secure.

You tear off the lock and begin to hoist up the metal security cage just enough to slip inside, then lower it behind you quietly. Hopefully, the creature won't even realize you're here.

As if to confirm this suspicion, you hear a horrific gurgling roar in the distance, echoing out down the mall corridors. It sounds like what was once the unicorn security guard is now far away.

You've successfully thrown off his trail.

Unfortunately, as you turn to face the inside of The Sport Spot, you find yourself with a whole other slew of problems.

The entire store is covered in sticky black tar, the substance growing out over the equipment, floor and walls as a toxic mold. Upon this new surface are dozens of large, egg-like pods, standing straight up and covered in thick, dark veins.

The air in here is a haze of drifting particles, the flakes dancing around like ash in the wind. They might be spores of some kind, floating in a matter that's similar to pollen. Fortunately, they remain focused in the middle of the store, and can't quite reach you as you stand over here on the edge.

You also notice that, at the back of the shop, through the black glittering mist and around the frighteningly large eggs, is a door to the mall concourse.

You have the necktie and will wrap it around your nose and mouth before creeping to the exit on page 69

You don't have the necktie but will take your chances creeping to the exit anyway on page 71

Head back out into the mall on page 57

You decide the food court is a great place to start your search for a safe exit. Behind these restaurants there must be one, or several, loading docks that lead to the outside world.

You begin to turn and walk away, when suddenly you hear a single, sharp tap. It sounds like someone is poking the nearby glass with a stick.

You look back and gasp in shock when you see what's waiting for you, a single enormous crab that stands just outside the food court, gazing through a single pane of the enormous glass wall. The creature as about the size of a large dog, with three sharp appendages on either side used for scuttling around, and two mighty pincers in the front. Its shell is black, with dark grey markings, and leaks a bubbling, tarlike ooze. The liquid drips out of the monster's carapace at a steady pace, covering the cement around it in haphazard splatters.

The monster begins to hiss and gurgle as you lock eyes with it, Voidal sludge continuing to pour forth from its mouth. It reaches up and taps the glass again with its claw, attempting to open its pincers wide enough to cut through.

Unfortunately for the crab, this simply cannot be done from any angle. Instead, the beast is forced to try breaking in by tapping with its giant sharp appendage, which isn't quite powerful enough to get the job done.

You let out a sigh of relief, but it doesn't last long.

Soon, you begin to see more of these horrific crustaceans scampering out from their hiding places across the parking lot, rushing over to the glass wall of the food court and tapping on the glass in a similar fashion. In the distance, you can even see more toxic crabs pouring out from the nearby woods.

While one of these creatures can't break through the glass on its own, several of them probably can, and you're not interested in sticking around long enough to find out for yourself.

You turn your attention back to the food court and take note that, while most of the restaurants are shuttered, it appears Ben's Burger Barn, The Chocolate Milk Man and The Spaghetti Hut are still unlocked.

62

It's likely that whoever was in charge of closing up at these places had to leave quickly.

Investigate The Spaghetti Hut on page 75
Investigate The Chocolate Milk Man on page 65
Investigate Ben's Burger Barn on page 148

Desperate times call for desperate measures, and right now you're in danger.

You walk back a bit and grab one of the many hard, metal-legged chairs that cover this food court, then dragged it over to the multi-paned glass wall that leads directly to your freedom.

You don't hesitate, gripping the chair tight then hurling it towards one of the windows as hard as you can.

There's a loud crash as the chair erupts through the translucent pane, shards blasting out across the cement parking lot like thousands of glittering lights in the evening glow.

Not wasting any time, you step out into the cool, fresh air and begin to hustle toward your car in a crouched position. You're hyper aware of your surroundings, eyes darting from vehicle to vehicle as you struggle to determine where the creature has hidden.

Soon enough, you arrive at your car, pulling out your keys and unlocking the door with one swift movement. You pull open the door and slide inside, immediately attempting to start it up and then gasping aloud as the engine struggles to roll over.

Sweat forming on your brow as your anxiety builds, you try one more time, listening with utter dread as the engine coughs and sputters, but fails to start.

"No, no, no," you stammer, slamming your hands against the dashboard.

Of course, you're not one to give up that easily.

Quickly switching gears, you pop your hood and swiftly climb out of the vehicle, hustling around to the front. You lift the hood and once again reel in shock at what's revealed within.

The innards of your car have been ripped to shreds, wires slashed and components torn and bent beyond recognition. There are deep, jagged claw marks everywhere, and the whole mess is covered in sticky black tar.

Suddenly, you hear a loud scuttling noise from behind.

You spin around to see not one, but a whole swarm of enormous Void crabs rushing towards you on their powerful, sharp limbs, tumbling over one another as they snap their claws and vomit forth disgusting belches of the toxic ooze. They're the size of large dogs, and move at a terrifyingly similar speed, standing between you and the forest that surrounds the mall parking lot. As far as you know, your escape back towards the food court is unguarded.

With little time to think about your next move, you spring into action.

Try to run past the Void crabs (I have a baseball bat) on page 108
Try to run past the Void crabs (I don't have a bat, but I'm light on my feet) on page 144
Run back towards the mall on page 137

The Chocolate Milk Man restaurant is still wide open, but the man himself is nowhere to be found. Or is he?

"Hey!" a voice suddenly hisses from behind the counter as you approach, instantly grabbing your attention.

You glance down to see the chocolate milk man, who happens to be an enormous, sentient carton of chocolate milk, is hiding behind the counter with a pressurized spray can held tightly in his hands.

"What is that?" you question.

The chocolate milk man holds the can so you can see its label. "Anti-Voidal Milk Spray," he informs you. "Anything from the endless cosmic Void gets near me and I'm spraying it right in the face."

"I don't know if that's gonna stop what's coming," you offer. "We've gotta get out of here."

Stoically, the sentient beverage shakes his head, refusing your offer. "I'll take my chances."

He doesn't seem to understand how serious the danger really is. "One can of Anti-Voidal spray isn't nearly enough," you plead. "You've gotta leave."

You hear the glass at the other end of the food court starting to crack, the force of the Void crabs struggling to get in weighing too heavy against the panes now. It's only a matter of time before they shatter completely and the creatures begin pouring in.

The living chocolate milk just shakes his head, steadfast in his decision. "Don't think I'm taking this lightly," he continues. "I've worked my whole life to get this business off the ground. I'm not about to leave it just because some crustaceans from another world are scampering around. I've put too much love into this restaurant to just cut and run."

You understand, but it's still difficult to accept what the chocolate milk man is saying. He's the honorable captain on a sinking ship, and there's something to be said for that, but there's also something to be said for getting out while you can.

Still, it's his decision to make.

The glass across the food court begins to crack again, and as you glance back over your shoulder you see web-like lines forming across multiple sections. There's not much time.

"The loading door out back is stuck," the chocolate milk man informs you, offering as much help as he can. He takes a ring of MALL KEYS off his belt and hands them to you. "You won't be able to get out through the food court, but the rest of the stores connect to a concourse that surrounds the mall. If you can make it to the back hallway you can probably find a way out. These keys might be able to help you."

You take the keys and start to reply, but the chocolate milk man cuts you off.

"Go!" he shouts. "There's not much time!"

Heed his words and head to the central hub on page 143

As you sprint toward the bright, flashing lights of Brain Drain Video Games you see that the metallic, rolling security cage has been left wide open.

"Become me!" the monster behind you bellows, gnashing its teeth and snapping the air with its mighty pinchers.

Your feet slamming hard against the floor and your breathing heavy, you notice the security cage spring to life, beginning its slow, automated descent downward. The timing is strangely perfect, as though intentionally planned to fall between you are the beast that's right behind you.

So long as you can keep up the pace.

The creature is close on your heels, but it's not quite fast enough to catch up with you as you push forth one final burst of speed. With all the energy you can muster, you drop to the smooth tile floor of the mall, sliding under the metal cage just as it closes behind you.

You jump in alarm as monster who was once a unicorn security guard slams against the metal with a deafening rattle.

The creature hisses and screeches, reaching out for you with its tentacles and claws through slits in the cage. However, it's much too large to get through, and not quite strong enough to break the whole thing down.

You watch in awe as the monster continues to push against the metal, however, and soon enough you find yourself lost in a trance, gazing past the gaping maw of this beast and into the infinite cosmos beyond.

"Yes, feast upon the knowledge. Understand the beginning and the end. Understand your decay," the creature moans in the voice of a thousand collapsing stars.

You can feel your mind flooding with information that no mortal should ever attempt to understand, and the sensation is intoxicating. Somehow, though, you know to pull away.

With every bit of discipline you can muster, you tear your gaze away from the beast, shutting your eyes tight and thinking of anything else.

You picture a dancing triceratops in a jacket and tie, with no pants and a winning smile. You picture a car with abs lounging by the pool. You picture a long walk through the park with a tall glass of chocolate milk in your hand.

Eventually, the squeals and hisses dissipate. The monster pulls away from the metal grate, disappointed that its prey has won this round. It stumbles off in the direction from which it came, a bubbling mess of mouths, tentacles, eyes, limbs and claws.

"I predicted with ninety-four point six percent certainty you'd need a place to escape," comes a computerized voice from all around you, drifting in through Brain Drain Video Game's public announcement system. It's the store's highly advanced artificial intelligence system, personifying itself with a smiling digital face that flickers to life on a small television screen behind the front counter.

"Thank you," you gush. "That was close."

"Not really," the computer continues. "The percentage of it catching you is very low under these particular circumstances."

You suddenly realize how helpful all this information could be in regard to your escape.

"What do I do now?" you blurt. "What's the safest path?"

The artificial intelligence system calculates for a moment, humming and whirring.

"Your likelihood of survival goes up exponentially if you head into the concourse with a numerical code," the computerized voice explains through the speakers above. "The door is in the back of this store. Remember the code number 4711."

Suddenly, there's a thunderous slam against the metallic roll cage, causing you to cry out in alarm. The creature is back, and his belligerent rage is even worse than before.

"You should go," the artificial intelligence informs you. "It is unlikely he will break through the security cage, but not impossible."

"Thank you," you gush, then hurry toward the exit.

Enter the mall concourse on page 90

You pull out the necktie you bought for your son, turning it around and pulling back a small flap to reveal a tiny fabric tag. Just like you thought, this has been treated to make it resistant to the Void.

Of course, who knows just how resistant it is, but at this point there's only one way to find out.

You take the tie and wrap it tightly around your face, not only covering your nose and your mouth, but angling the fabric in such a way that it covers your ears as well. There's no reason to take any chances.

Once you've prepared yourself, you take a deep draw of air and hold it in, only adding to your multiple layers of precaution before entering this hazardous area.

It's about fifty feet from here to the back of the store, which isn't so far that you'll have any trouble holding your breath, but there's also the many egg pods to maneuver around.

Senses on high alert, you walk briskly out onto the surface of toxic Voidal sludge. You're lucky you didn't try this at a full sprint, because the second you touch it, you realize just how slippery the mess below your feet really is.

You wobble a bit, but quickly regain your balance.

As you move through the haze, the particles float past you innocuously enough, but about halfway through the area you find yourself feeling incredibly light headed. Just two more steps, and your sense of balance gives way, causing you to stumble a bit. You catch yourself before going down completely.

Fortunately, your necktie has filtered out most of the toxins, allowing you to quickly regain your focus and continue onward. You shudder to think what might've happened without this fabric over your face, though.

As you reach the other side, you begin to hear a plethora of strange and unexpected sounds from behind you. There are several quick, wet pops as the egg pods begin to open up, blooming like horrific flowers. You glance over your shoulder very quickly to see tiny Void crabs beginning to emerge by the hundreds, scuttling after you on their tiny legs. By then you're already opening the door to the concourse and slamming it shut behind you.

70

The seal is airtight. You're safe.

Explore the concourse on page 90

With nothing to protect your face and lungs, your options are limited, but right now anything sounds better than turning around and heading back in the direction you came from.

It's about fifty feet from here to the back of the store, which isn't so far that you'll have any trouble holding your breath. Still, without knowing exactly what these strange floating particles are, its hard to tell if this technique will even matter.

There's also the many egg pods to maneuver around.

You take a deep breath and hold it, then walk briskly out onto the surface of toxic Voidal sludge. You're lucky you didn't try this at a full sprint, because the second you touch it, you realize just how slippery this mess below your feet really is.

You wobble a bit, but quickly regain your balance.

As you move through the haze, the particles float past you innocuously enough, but about halfway through the area you find yourself feeling incredibly light headed. Just two more steps, and your sense of balance gives way, causing you to stumble a bit. You catch yourself before going down completely, but moment's later your knees give out under the weight of your body.

You slam hard against the ground, the air bursting forth from your lungs as you sputter and gasp. As you inhale again, you witness the spores as they're pulled through the air and into your body, the tiny flakes burning your lungs.

This effect only causes you to cough and gasp more, and soon enough you're completely overwhelmed by the toxic, noxious air. You can feel yourself getting weaker and weaker, until eventually you can't move at all, frozen in place in a contorted, horrific position right there on the floor.

You're panicking now, but regardless of the frantic effort you're putting in, your body refuses to react.

You can still see and hear, however.

There are several quick, wet pops as the egg pods begin to open up, blooming like strange flowers. You watch as tiny Void crabs begin to emerge by the hundreds, scuttling towards you on their tiny legs, hungry for their first meal.

THE END

"Please don't open that door," you beg the triceratops as sternly and earnestly as possible. "There's a tidal wave of Void ooze waiting right outside."

This causes the dinosaur to hesitate, but not because she believes you. Instead, she seems to be taken aback by the sheer audacity of your claim.

"I've caught a lot of troublemakers back here and they've feed me plenty of bullshit stories," she offers, "but this is a new one."

"I'm not lying," you plead. "There was a timeline tear... or something. I don't really know, but whatever it was, it opened up pathway for The Void to spill out into this reality."

The triceratops narrows her eyes. "The timeline tear out by the lake?" she questions. "It was on the news. They said it was handled."

"Well, it wasn't," you inform her.

The dinosaur shakes her head, clearly not believing you. "Timeline tears are harmless," she scoffs, then yanks the door open.

The second this door is free from the bolt that's keeping it closed it erupts wide with a powerful slam, tossing the triceratops back across the room as a flood of jet black liquid comes crashing after her.

Without a moment to spare, you turn and leap into the vent, just barely grabbing onto the ledge and hoisting yourself up. Unfortunately, *ANY ITEMS* that you're carrying fall into the bubbling toxic ooze as you do this. They are no longer in your possession.

Safely in the vent, you look back over your shoulder to see that the room is already halfway full of the horrific sludge. You can see three horns covered in ooze just barely break the surface, then submerge once again as they disappear completely.

Your heart breaks for the dinosaur, but there's not time to waist. You begin to climb up into the vent.

Crawl to the rooftop on page 3

Realizing that you don't know the passcode for the door on your right, nor have the keys for the door on your left, you immediately fly into a state of panic. You begin to slam your hands against them, creating a frantic cacophony of sound as the tidal wave of Voidal tar looms closer.

When this doesn't work, you turn your attention to the locks themselves, kicking them with as much force as you can possibly muster.

Unfortunately, these security measures were specifically designed to stop this kind of thing, and your efforts are useless.

The wall of bubbling Void tar slams into you, completely enveloping your body in a black wave. Your head is instantly submerged, and the force of this flood knocks you off your feet. You're tumbling now, but for some strange reason you don't smash into the wall behind you. Instead, you just continue to roll end over end through the chaotic sea of sludge, the darkness surrounding you in an ever expanding cosmic space.

Eventually, your movements begin to slow. You gradually slip into a slow drift, gliding through a vast empty space that is completely foreign.

Your eyes had been shut tight this whole time, and when you finally open them you feel no pain. In fact, it feels as though you're not surrounded by liquid at all.

This expanse is one where space and time are non-existent, a reality at the edge of all we know and understand, and one that continues well beyond this limit.

Before you, the ghosts of dying stars begin to groan, their cosmic drone pulsing through your flesh in notes that no human ears should ever hear. These are the songs that were never written, the melodies that cannot be, and as they enter your mind they're both enchanting and painful.

You can't stop listening and learning, however. Instead of pulling away from this vast understanding, you push deeper into it, allowing yourself to accept everything it has to offer.

You can feel your mind opening wider and wider, tearing itself apart from within, but you don't care at all. You allow yourself to dissolve into The Void.

THE END

Something is definitely wrong here, but your curiosity is still much stronger than the looming sense of dread. Your heart slamming within your chest, you slowly begin to creep around the counter and make your way back to the prep kitchen.

You push through the door carefully, your senses on high alert as you continue onward. The second you cross the threshold you spot Ben, the owner of Ben's Burger Barn, standing with his back to you on the other side of the room.

The toxic scent is even more pungent in here, almost overwhelming, and you instinctually wrinkle your nose.

Ben doesn't turn to greet you, in fact he doesn't even look up. Instead, he remains focused on his work, chopping away with a large cleaver at something that sits on the counter before him. From this angle, you can't quite see what it is, but as you step closer the tension and anxiety within you does nothing but build.

"I'm working on a new menu," Ben calls out, apparently aware of your presence. "There are so many great ingredients at the mall if you know where to look!"

You step a little closer and see now that the counter Ben's working upon is covered in black, bubbling tar, the liquid spilling over onto the floor in long dripping strands. Even more disturbing is the new ingredient at this man's disposal. You gasp aloud as you realize that the chef is hacking away at a large, disconnected dinosaur tail, cutting the reptilian segment into an assortment of disc-like portions.

"Oh my god," you stammer, stepping back as you reel in horror.

You don't make it far, however, slamming into something behind you with a deep thud. You turn around to see the unicorn security guard, or what's left of him. The once familiar horned officer has transformed completely, his entire head opening up like a set of enormous jaws. Tentacles and claws have burst out from within this hollow shell, black ooze spilling everywhere as his voice bubbles out from the toxic mess.

"You shouldn't be back here!" the creature screeches.

Before you have a chance you react, the unicorn's new jaws snap down onto you with a ferocious bite.

THE END

The Spaghetti Hut is empty, but it's still not closed and locked for the evening. Your dear friend who is typically working here, Batoon the bigfoot, is nowhere to be found. She must've left once she noticed things getting strange.

You creep up to the counter and peer over the edge, making sure that none of these vicious Voidal crabs have somehow gotten inside and are lying in wait.

Nothing's back there, and you breathe a sigh of relief. So far so good.

You continue onward, sneaking behind the counter and making your way towards another door, which leads to the prep kitchen.

"Hello?" you call out. "Is anybody there?"

There's no response.

You push through the door and find yourself standing in a room full of uncooked pasta and bottle upon bottle of spaghetti sauce. If the situation wasn't currently so dire, you'd likely be in heaven right now, but there's no time to stop and daydream about all of that delicious spaghetti.

Your bigfoot friend is still nowhere to be found, but you do notice a set of keys hanging on a hook nearby. Above them is a label that says MALL KEYS, and you take them immediately. Who knows when these might come in handy.

Before you is the door to the loading docks, and as you continue toward it you suddenly get a very bad feeling. From the food court behind, a sharp cracking sound erupts as the crabs begin to heave against the glass, testing the limits before it breaks entirely and the horrific creatures come pouring through.

You barely notice. Instead, your eyes remain glued on the door to the loading docks, your mind racing with questions about what could lie beyond.

You slowly open the door, finding that this new room is pitch black. You reach your hand around on the wall next to you, searching for a light switch and flicking it on.

Nothing happens. The power must be cut in here.

"Hello?" you call out into the darkness, not really expecting a response but doing it out of habit.

"Hello?" a voice suddenly calls back, their tone strangely familiar.

"Who's there?" you continue.

The voice yells back to you from the darkness in turn, matching your cadence almost exactly. "Who's there?"

There's another loud crack from the food court glass behind you. The windows are about to give way, and soon enough the crabs will be pouring through in as a hissing, pulsing swarm. There's no time to check out the other restaurants, but if you leave now you can probably make it to the central hub before it's too late.

Get the heck out of here on page 143
Continue into the darkness on page 40

"And they just started exploding?" your son's friend, Heather, questions. "Popping like balloons?"

You shake your head. "More like collapsing into piles of dust," you offer. "It was still wild."

It's your son's birthday, but right now all the attention is on you. Your son's friends have packed the dining room, where you sit on a chair in the middle of the crowd and field questions about your wild night at The Billings Mall. Everyone had been following the nightly news, locked down in their homes while your adventure unfolded at the heart of the action.

They want to know all the details, and you're happy to give them up, so long as it doesn't take away from the real reason you're all gathered here today. Fortunately, your son seems just as interested as everyone else does.

"Did you actually see the security guard change?" Pete, another one of your son's friends questions. "You saw him grow claws and tentacles and stuff?"

"He was chasing me through the mall when it happened," you offer. "I saw the whole thing."

The crowd gasps.

"But, I'm no hero," you continue. "Anyone else would've done what I did."

Now it's time for your son to step up. He places his hand lovingly on your shoulder. "You were doing what you thought was right, but not everyone would've made it back here in one piece. You made a lot of important choices along the way and look where it brought you."

You smile reluctantly.

"You're a hero," your son reaffirms.

There's nothing more flattering than the way he's looking up to you right now, and you find yourself getting very emotional. Before it gets to far, however, you realize this is a perfect time to shaft gears.

"I'm not the one we should be celebrating today," you blurt, changing the subject. "My son is one year older and one year wiser!"

Everyone applauds, hooting and hollering as your son smiles.

"Let's get the gifts started," someone calls out from the crowd.

"You go first," Heather chimes in, nodding in your direction.

If you don't have a gift turn to page 139
If you got him a baseball bat turn to page 130
If you got him a video game turn to page 44
If you got him a necktie turn to page 134
If you got him a book turn to page 135

As frightening as this situation is, you muster up all the discipline you can manage and remain calm. Right now, the unicorn security guard still has some deep, uncorrupted part of his mind that's telling him to help you, regardless of the other toxic messages tumbling around in there.

Who knows how long this good fortune could last, but you'll cross that bridge when you come to it. Right now, you just need to get back into the mall and away from this ever growing swarm of gurgling Void crabs.

Eventually, the vehicle pulls to the shattered glass hole that you'd originally left from, parking just close enough for you to climb out of the car and back into the mall. From here, it would be difficult for any large crabs to follow through, at least until the security guard pulls away. This gives you a brief window of time to protect yourself.

"Vandals," the unicorn security guard observes. "Leaving their mark on a world that is in constant decay. Calling out to be noticed in a frothing sea of maggots."

"Uh... yeah," you reply with a nod. "Thanks again for the ride."

The unicorn says nothing, just remains frozen in place as he stares at the broken window. He remains like this long enough for you to finally turn and carefully open the car door, slinking out and shutting it behind you. Through the window you can still see the unicorn security guard staring off into space, utterly frozen.

Without another moment's hesitation, you grab one of the nearby food court tables. The thing is twice as heavy as you'd expect, which is both good and bad given the circumstances. While you have a hell of a time dragging it over to the opening, you know that once it's in position you'll have some space to figure out what's next.

You begin to lift the table, groaning loudly as your muscles strain. You're giving it everything you've got, pushing with all your might as the car finally pulls away.

Fortunately, you manage to close the gap just in time, the table tipping forward just enough to keep it propped against the opening you've created.

There are small spaces in between that the Void crabs reach their pinchers through, snapping their claws frantically in the air, but they're too large to get their whole bodies inside, especially with their hard, wide shells to contend with.

The creatures begin to spread out a bit, tapping on the glass the covers the entire food court wall as they test their options. This seems to hold them at bay for now, but as you watch you can see more of these horrific abominations emerging from the distant forest, rushing over to join their friends.

You can tell just from observing them that the crabs are not particularly smart, and figure their need to get inside might be driven entirely by some hunter's instinct. They don't know the mall is empty, they're just looking for food.

Of course, there's at least one unfortunate soul still left inside. Lucky you.

Return to the central hub and look for another way out on page 143
Investigate the food court and look for another way out on page 61

As stress continues to overwhelm your body, you decide the best treatment is to bathe yourself in the smooth sounds of The Top Pop Hits with Brindle Creems, a daily rundown of all Montana's hottest chart topping tunes.

You quickly flip your radio dial over to the local pop station, and are met with the familiar voice of Brindle Creems himself.

"That was Borb and The Orbs with their newest single, 'I Want Your Milk'. Now we're entering the top five with a little number I've been humming all day to be perfectly honest. I wouldn't be surprised if this one continues to climb the charts because it's as catchy as they get, and who doesn't enjoy a song about love! It's a beautiful evening out there in Montana so lets turn it up with the sweet sounds of Martha Moobin and her killer new track, 'Love Is Real!'"

Suddenly, a hammering synthesizer bass begins to rumble through your car speakers, followed shortly thereafter by the pulsing beat of this powerful anthem. You begin to nod your head along to the sound, your anxiety melting away as a glowing smile begins to creep its way across your face. You've never heard this song before, but it's already filling you with a warm feeling of positivity and excitement for whatever comes next.

There's no question that you're going to find the perfect birthday gift for your son.

The vocals begin, Martha Moobin's formidable voice dancing across the track below it in a triumphant, soaring cadence. "Love is real! Love is true! From buckaroo to buckaroo!" she sings. These words begin to repeat over and over again, until eventually you find yourself joining in without thinking twice.

The next thing you know, you're belting it out at the top of your lungs, repeating the chorus of Martha Moobin's gorgeous hit song in confident repetition.

Suddenly, however, everything changes. Without warning, a small object darts out of the forest and into the road, causing you to grab the wheel tight and swerve to the left. You slam on your breaks as the sound of a grinding squeal erupts through the air around you.

You're now stopped in the middle of the road, no other cars as far as the eye can see and the sound of pop music still blaring in your ears. You quickly reach over and turn off the radio as you struggle to collect yourself.

At first you're not entirely sure you've avoided the object, whatever it was. Looking in the rearview mirror, however, reveals the road behind you is now empty.

From the corner of your eye, you spot something scuttling off into the forest, a large black object that's low to the ground. You're not entirely sure, but it appears to be moving with the help of several sharp, insect-like appendages, but from this distance it's difficult to tell.

Before your mind can even begin to understand what you're looking at, it's already gone.

You take a deep breath and let it out. In any other situation you'd probably pull off onto the side of the road and sit for a moment, but the dashboard clock serves as a constant reminder of just how little time you have left. The mall is closing soon, and you can't let whatever this unexpected creature was put a stop to the mission at hand.

You eventually put the car back into drive and continue on your way, this time in complete silence.

Soon enough, you're arriving at the Billings Mall, pulling off the road and into the parking lot.

Continue to The Billings Mall on page 13

The food court is now completely empty, any mall patrons already cleared out for the evening and the workers finished with their duties. There's an eerie feeling in the air, and it's not helped by the fact that the music which typically pumps in over the mall public announcement system has changed slightly, now strange and distorted. The once familiar upbeat song crackles and pops, speeding up and slowing down at random intervals as though spilling out through a sonic butter churn.

You keep up the pace, heading straight for the front doors and then slamming into them hard, rattling the glass as you stumble back in shock.

You try again, with slightly less force this time, and once more find yourself rejected by the unmoving frame. Further investigation reveals that the door has been locked, jammed shut with a metal bar that was then completely snapped off.

You can't tell if whoever did this was trying to keep someone in, or out.

The entire wall of this portion of the mall is constructed from large glass windowpanes, allowing the food court to receive and ample amount of light. From your position, you can gaze out through the glass, noticing that a few scattered cars remain in the lot.

You can see your own vehicle sitting right where you left it, tempting you with freedom.

Suddenly, you reel in alarm, catching a glimpse of something small and black scuttling quickly between two of the cars.

"What the fuck," you blurt, peering out through the glass in hopes of getting a better look.

Whatever it is, it's left a long trail of black ooze in its path. You can see now that this bubbling, toxic tar is splattered in various locations across the cement.

Your heart slamming hard within your chest, you struggle to determine the best course of action. One thing's for sure, something very strange is afoot, and this once familiar setting of The Billings Mall is no longer safe.

84

Already knowing what will happen, you try and push through the door one last time. It still doesn't budge, and now you're left with some very tough decisions to make.

To break the glass and head out to your car, turn to page 63
Return to the mall's central hub and look for another way out from there on page 143
Head to the food court and look for another way out on page 61

You grab ahold of the blue tarp and quickly wrap it around the end of your metal pole, then hoist this creation up into the air. You wave it frantically back and forth, doing everything you can to attract the attention of the helicopter above.

At first it seems hopeless, as their focus remains on sending bolts of magically concentrated love down into the swarming Void creatures. Eventually, however, you spot one of the wizards pointing in your direction, yelling out to someone else in the vehicle who's wearing a dark Anti-Voidal Task Force uniform.

The two of them exchange quite a few words, continuing to point at you while you jump up and down with excitement.

The man in the uniform pulls out a set of binoculars and places them over his eyes for a better look. He stays like this for a good while and then suddenly pulls them away, nodding his head in confirmation.

The helicopter immediately alters course, swooping around and taking a direct route to your location on the roof. You watch as a ladder is tossed from the side of the vehicle, snaking down towards you as the air begins to rush past.

The blades are loud and unnerving, but soon another sound enters your ears, this one much more frightening than the hum of a helicopter.

You turn around to see that several winged Void crabs have scuttled over the edge of the rooftop. They have you in their sights and immediately begin to flutter in your direction with their teeth bared and their pinchers snapping.

With seconds to spare, the first rung of the ladder finally reaches your hand, and you grab onto it tightly as the helicopter begins to lift off.

Your feet leave the ground, but these creatures are just as capable of flight as you are. One of the Void crabs lunges at you, its claws extended, but just before he gets a chance to grip your flesh a bolt of magical energy flies past you and smashes into the monster. The Void crab is blown apart, his Voidal energy disintegrating and drifting away like ash in the wind.

Two more blasts of magic shoot past you from the wizard above, taking out another pair of Void crabs that are hot on your trail. Soon enough, the monsters are no longer following.

You gaze down at The Billings Mall as you float away, watching as the Anti-Voidal Task Force continues to close in.

86

You're exhausted, and you've got a big day tomorrow.

Get some rest and head to your son's birthday on page 118

After outrunning the security guard creature, you don't see how getting past a monstrous living dresser should be that difficult.

Immediately, you spring into action, dodging this way and that as the dresser continues to block your path. It's only once you start playing this game of cat and mouse that you realize how quick this thing moves, and how difficult it'll be to make it to safety.

Still, you have to try.

Finally, you make your move, sprinting as fast as you can around the dresser and bolting toward the exit door. You can hear the creature lumbering after you with it's thunderous footsteps, the sentient piece of furniture bounding over a mess of clothing as its tentacles whip the air behind you. You can feel their presence on the back of your neck, the creature just barely out of reach.

You hit the door running, grabbing the handle and yanking it back as hard as you can. The door opens wide, but unfortunately this split second is all it takes for the tentacle filled dresser to catch up with you.

The slimy, ooze covered appendages envelope your body, struggling to pull you away from the door as you grip its handle tight. Soon enough, you're being lifted off the ground, using every ounce of strength you have left to hold onto the door handle.

Gradually, however, your fingers begin to slip away from the metal, pulling off one by one.

You can feel the tentacles covering your entire body with their cold, Voidal embrace. You cry out, but there's nobody left in the mall to hear you. Moments later you're torn aware from the door, engulfed completely by the living dresser's lashing appendages.

THE END

Your expression falters slightly, but you quickly pull yourself together and straighten up. There's no reason to bring down the atmosphere of your son's party just because you couldn't manage to retrieve a gift for him.

"I actually... don't have a present this time," you stammer. "I'm sorry, buddy."

Your son smiles. He doesn't seem disappointed in the least. "That's okay, you had a big night. I'm just thankful you're alive after all that. The last thing you need to worry about is getting me a birthday present."

"It feels strange taking a trip to the mall and going through all that to end up with nothing," you reply.

"*The Void* is nothing," your son replies wisely. "You know that first hand. What's happening right now is... everything else."

You look around at all the smiling friends and family, quickly realizing your son is right. This is what matters. It would've been great to find him that perfect gift, but there are plenty of birthdays to come.

You hug your son. "I love you," you offer.

"I love you, too," he replies. "Thanks for making it back in one piece."

Suddenly, Pete calls out from the other room. "Hey, whose Mustang's jersey is that?"

At first, you're not quite sure what he's talking about, but as the crowd of revelers parts you see that Pete has discovered your makeshift red flag sitting crumpled by the door. He holds it up, letting the uniform unfurl.

"I found it at the mall," you reply. "That's what I used to make my rescue flag. I would've offered that up as a gift but it's too tattered and torn."

"Even in this condition it's worth *a lot* of money," Pete continues. "This is a real Hermpo Torms rookie uniform, and it's signed on the back. I don't think this is a replica."

The crowd gasps, although you're still not entirely sure what he's saying.

"This jersey is worth crazy amounts of money," Pete continues. "You're rich."

You stroll up to him and he hands you the Jersey, which you carry back over to your previous position. "I'm not rich," you offer in return. "My son is."

You hand over the uniform to your son, who can't believe his eyes when he sees the signature on the back.

"Happy birthday," you tell him.

THE END

You enter the mall concourse with caution, every sense trained and on high alert. You didn't make it this far through acting foolish, but through a series of carefully planned and plotted decisions.

This hallway is long and narrow, with a grey cement floor and white walls that have since faded with dirt, dust and grime. Much of the paint is chipped and flaking from various boxes slamming against it during deliveries.

The florescent lights above cast your surroundings in an eerie, otherworldly glow, their coloration just the slightest bit off as they flicker and sputter. With every change in luminescence they make a high pitched clicking sound, followed by an ominous hum.

This buzz isn't the only sound, however. From all around you can hear a constant dripping that echoes out through these seemingly endless corridors.

The dripping makes sense, though, as the only other prominent feature back here is the cluster of pipes that line the ceiling, running along the length of this hallway.

You continue to walk the concourse, taking note of the slight angle that guides it ever so slightly around the circumference of the mall.

While other sections of the hallway are lined with back entrances to a variety of shops, this portion is free from any of these features. You're likely behind one of the large department stores now.

As you round the bend, you suddenly find yourself face to face with the source of the dripping noise. At least, one of them.

A pipe has bent from its own internal pressure, leaking out onto the ground with a deeply concerning flow of black, Voidal tar. The ooze splatters across the cement below, creating a small pool.

You make sure to step around it cautiously, putting as much space between you and the substance as possible, but as you do this there's a mammoth rumble that courses through the building, rattling the light fixtures and causing the cluster of overhead pipes to groan.

The dripping liquid immediately begins to speed up, transforming from a quick drip to a constant stream.

You look up at the pipes, hearing them squeal again with even more ferocity. Something's very wrong here.

Suddenly, the pipes above you erupt with a loud clang as cascades of thick, toxic ooze begin to pour forth. You jump back in alarm, stumbling a bit as the liquid keeps coming and coming.

"Oh my god," you stammer, hardly believing your eyes as every single one of the pipes succumbs to the pressure, blasting forth with a flood of black toxic sludge.

There's so much of it spilling forth now that it's more like a wave than a leak, the Voidal ooze rushing towards you.

Immediately, you turn and begin to sprint down the hallway, moving as fast as you can while the stream of bubbling liquid follows close behind. You glance back over your shoulder to see that the waterline has risen, flowing higher and higher with every bursting pipe.

Soon enough, the end of the hallway comes into view. It's a flat white wall, with a door to the left and a door to the right. Both of these exits feature a lock, one in the form of a numerical keypad (which has a sign that says "air regulation" about it), and another in the form of a standard lock (which features a plaque with the word "security" emblazoned across it).

You have to act fast.

If you know the numerical pass, open that door on page 100
If you have the mall keys use them on page 95
If don't have the mall keys or the numerical pass turn to page 73

As wonderful as this reality is, you've still got a little more adventure left in you. After all, it's not every day that you get a chance to go back and check out other potential timelines you happened to miss during the first run through.

You'll be careful, and soon enough you'll be right back here on the couch where your started. Or ended. Honestly, you're not quite sure.

You flip to the first page of the book and begin to read as the world around you melts away. You watch as the walls peel back to reveal a universe passing by in reverse, the pathways of fate all curling back onto themselves.

"It's been a long day in Billings, but there's one very important stop left on your list," you read, the words flying from your lips at an incredible rate. "You're headed towards the mall in search of a gift for your son, as his 25th birthday is, technically speaking, just hours away."

You realize now that, in your excitement, you've been rushing the story.

You stop reading, and suddenly the meta loop comes to a screeching halt. You hear a loud tearing sound, as though a page is being torn from the very book that you hold in your hands.

You glance around to see that you're standing in a thick forest. To your right, the trees open up into a beautiful view of Lake Elmo. It's a glorious sight, but this isn't where you're supposed to be.

You take a deep breath and start over, careful not to rush things this time. You begin to read aloud.

Read from your book on page 1

Your eyes stay trained on the broken dresser and limp tentacles for a long while, searching for any tiny sign of life. You gaze so intently that, a few times, it seems like there *just might* have been a twitch or a shiver, but you quickly recognize the fact that your eyes are starting to play tricks on you.

After all, your heart is beating so hard within your chest that it feels as though it's shaking your entire body.

You'd love to just continue onward, to get as far away from this corrupted living object as quickly as you can, but deep down in the pit of your stomach you know that those keys are going to come in handy. If you don't make a move for them now, then you'll certainly regret it later.

Slowly, carefully, you reach your hand out for the key ring, your body ready to react and pull away at even the slightest sound or movement.

Closer and closer you creep, until finally your fingers wrap ever so slightly around the edge of the metal circle.

You pull them back quickly, the keys jingling a little more than you feel comfortable with. It was worth it, however. You now hold the MALL KEYS safely within your hands.

You back away from the monster, then eventually turn and head out through to back door of the store.

Enter the mall concourse on page 90

The numbers swirling within your mind finally coalesce into a four-digit code that feels right. Without another moment's hesitation, you enter this code and feel a sharp jolt of panic shoot through your body as a red flashing light appears, blinking the heart wrenching two-word message over and over again, "no entry".

The code is wrong.

The wall of bubbling, toxic tar slams into you, completely enveloping your body in a black wave. Your head is instantly submerged, and the force of this flood knocks you off your feet. You're tumbling now, but for some strange reason you don't crash into the wall behind you. Instead, you just continue to roll end over end through the chaotic sea of sludge, the darkness surrounding you in an ever expanding cosmic space.

Eventually, your movements begin to slow. You gradually slip into a slow drift, gliding through a vast empty space that is completely foreign to you.

Your eyes had been shut tight this whole time, and when you finally open them you feel no pain. In fact, it feels as though you're not surrounded by liquid at all.

This expanse is one where space and time are non-existent, a reality at the edge of all we know and understand, and one that continues well beyond this limit.

Before you, the ghosts of dying stars begin to groan, their cosmic drone pulsing through you in notes that no human ears should ever hear. These are the songs that were never written, the melodies that cannot be, and as they enter your mind they are both enchanting and painful.

You can't stop listening and learning, however. Instead of pulling away from this vast understanding, you push deeper into it, allowing yourself to accept everything that it has to offer.

You can feel your mind opening wider and wider, tearing itself apart from within, but you don't care at all. You allow yourself to dissolve into The Void.

THE END

The ring of mall keys has many options, and there's no way to discern which one of them works on this particular lock other than to try them all out. As the wave of Voidal ooze cascades towards you, there's only time for one or two attempts.

The first one fails.

"Oh shit, oh shit," you begin to mumble to yourself, flipping to the next key and then jamming it into the lock before you. You turn your wrist and immediately hear a loud hollow clang as the bolt slides clear, allowing you access.

You throw open the door and dive inside, slamming it behind you not a moment too soon. The second you're sealed off you can hear the crash of raging liquid hitting the back wall of the hallway, completely filling the concourse with a seemingly endless flood of toxic tar.

Your breathing heavy, you take a brief moment to collect yourself, then turn around to examine your new surroundings.

You're standing in the unicorn security guard's private office. There's a row of filing cabinets, as well as a locker and a desk. Atop the desk sits a computer that has been smashed to pieces by some large object, and next to it is a half eaten burger from Ben's Burger Shack.

What's left of the food has quickly evolved. Half the burger has quickly decayed and transformed into a grotesque, black mutation. There's are small tentacle-like growths that now protruded from the infected half, swaying from side to side in the air as though waving in a breeze that isn't there.

This, however, is not the most noteworthy thing in the office. On the other side of the desk is a radio that's loudly blasting the static of The Snow Channel. While you typically enjoy this kind of thing, the blaring hum is already giving you a splitting headache.

Turn off the radio on page 101
Change the channel to the news on page 119
Change The channel to The Top Pop Hits with Brindle Creems to lighten the mood on page 102

The numbers swirling within your mind finally coalesce into a four-digit code that feels right. Without another moment's hesitation, you enter this code and feel a sharp jolt of panic shoot through your body as a red flashing light appears, blinking the heart wrenching two-word message over and over again, "no entry".

The code is wrong.

The wall of bubbling, toxic tar slams into you, completely enveloping your body in a black wave. Your head is instantly submerged, and the force of this flood knocks you off your feet. You're tumbling now, but for some strange reason you don't crash into the wall behind you. Instead, you just continue to roll end over end through the chaotic sea of sludge, the darkness surrounding you in an ever expanding cosmic space.

Eventually, your movements begin to slow. You gradually slip into a slow drift, gliding through a vast empty space that is completely foreign to you.

Your eyes had been shut tight this whole time, and when you finally open them you feel no pain. In fact, it feels as though you're not surrounded by liquid at all.

This expanse is one where space and time are non-existent, a reality at the edge of all we know and understand, and one that continues well beyond this limit.

Before you, the ghosts of dying stars begin to groan, their cosmic drone pulsing through you in notes that no human ears should ever hear. These are the songs that were never written, the melodies that cannot be, and as they enter your mind they are both enchanting and painful.

You can't stop listening and learning, however. Instead of pulling away from this vast understanding, you push deeper into it, allowing yourself to accept everything that it has to offer.

You can feel your mind opening wider and wider, tearing itself apart from within, but you don't care at all. You allow yourself to dissolve into The Void.

THE END

You decide the most practical gift for your son is a tie, and make a direct line towards Fashion Forward, which also happens to be one of his favorite shops in the mall.

As you approach, you notice the roll-down metal security cage has already been shut, but there's still a bit of movement within the establishment, and this gives you the tiniest sliver of hope. Maybe whoever is working this evening will open things back up for you if you promise to shop quickly.

You arrive at the shutter and now have a much better view inside. You can see that the figure moving within is actually a living dresser, who is currently taking a moment to tidy up the store before fully closing down for the evening.

"Hey!" you call out. "I'm so sorry to do this, but is there any way you could let me buy a tie from you? I know that I'm a little behind but... it's my son's birthday."

The sentient piece of furniture turns and begins to approach you. At first, you can see that he's smiling wide, a very good sign, but moment's later the dresser's expression suddenly falters.

He's looking at you now with deep concern and, strangely, fear. You don't have a mirror in front of you, but you can only assume that you don't appear to be in the best health right now.

"I'm sorry, I can't help you," the dresser replies sternly.

"I know exactly what I want," you plead. "In and out in five seconds."

The sentient piece of furniture just continues to stare, horrified and confused. He seems lost in a trance for a brief moment, taking in your appearance, but he quickly snaps out of it.

"You should go," is all the dresser says in return. "There's probably a few stores still open."

You begin to protest, but before you can finish the living furniture turns and heads back into his store. He gets about ten steps and then stops, taking one last peak at you over his shoulder before continuing on his way.

98

Maybe you can catch another shop before they shutter, but you'd better hurry.

Head to The Sport Spot on page 36

Head to Brain Drain Video Games on page 9

Head to Books For Buds on page 132

The numbers swirling within your mind finally coalesce into a four-digit code that feels right. Without another moment's hesitation, you enter this code and feel a sharp jolt of panic shoot through your body as a red flashing light appears, blinking the heart wrenching two-word message over and over again, "no entry".

The code is wrong.

The wall of bubbling, toxic tar slams into you, completely enveloping your body in a black wave. Your head is instantly submerged, and the force of this flood knocks you off your feet. You're tumbling now, but for some strange reason you don't crash into the wall behind you. Instead, you just continue to roll end over end through the chaotic sea of sludge, the darkness surrounding you in an ever expanding cosmic space.

Eventually, your movements begin to slow. You gradually slip into a slow drift, gliding through a vast empty space that is completely foreign to you.

Your eyes had been shut tight this whole time, and when you finally open them you feel no pain. In fact, it feels as though you're not surrounded by liquid at all.

This expanse is one where space and time are non-existent, a reality at the edge of all we know and understand, and one that continues well beyond this limit.

Before you, the ghosts of dying stars begin to groan, their cosmic drone pulsing through you in notes that no human ears should ever hear. These are the songs that were never written, the melodies that cannot be, and as they enter your mind they are both enchanting and painful.

You can't stop listening and learning, however. Instead of pulling away from this vast understanding, you push deeper into it, allowing yourself to accept everything that it has to offer.

You can feel your mind opening wider and wider, tearing itself apart from within, but you don't care at all. You allow yourself to dissolve into The Void.

THE END

You remember that the password to thid door is 7411... or was it 4711?

You glance behind you to see that the mass of Voidal tar is just seconds from sweeping you away. You need to act fast, but as you turn your attention back to this numerical lock your mind floods with various possibilities.

Sevens, sixes, fives and fours dance within your mind, pulling your attention this way and that as you struggle to determine the correct answer. You'd made a mental note to keep this information close to the surface of your mind, but so much has happened since then.

Still, you have a vague idea of where to begin.

You decide to punch in your code.

Enter code 4117 on page 94
Enter code 4711 on page 42
Enter code 7411 on page 96
Enter code 7144 on page 99

You love The Snow Channel, but right now there's too much on your mind to understand the messages between the static. You reach out and turn off the radio, plunging the room into sweet, sweet silence.

The only sound now is the soft lapping of liquid as the Voidal ooze that fills the hallway rocks against the closed office door. You glance down to see that, although this door its quite tight, it doesn't seal off completely. A small black pool is starting to form on the floor, prompting you onward.

There's not much time.

You glance around the room a little more to see there are two vent openings near the ceiling, but they're large enough for you to fit through and the screws that hold their covers in place appear to be loose. If you climb up onto the desk, you should have no trouble getting inside.

There's a map of The Billings Mall hanging on the wall next to you, and after taking a moment to study it, you determine that one of these vents leads to the rooftop, while the other will take you to the mall manager's office.

Crawl in rooftop vent on page 3
Crawl in manager's office vent on page 7

102

You change the radio over to your local pop music station, hoping to elevate the mood a bit after so much danger and drama.

"Welcome back! I'm Brindle Creems here in Billings, Montana, providing you with the best pop songs of the day that'll have you tapping your toes and singing from your heart. We're gonna do something a little unusual here on the countdown, because it's an unusual kinda night here in The Love State. I've been getting so many calls from listeners about Martha Moobin's new track, 'Love Is Real', that I'm gonna dedicate this hour to the track. That's right, nothing other than 'Love Is Real!' Let's go!"

Heavy synthesizer bass begins to rattle through the speakers, causing a smile to immediately appear on your face. You can see why so many people have been calling in about this track. It's really, really good.

The second this song begins to play, you notice that the tentacles sprouting from the cheeseburger on the security guard's desk begin to tremble and shake, pulling away from the source of the music in a frantic tangle.

Suddenly, it all clicks. If there's one thing the tune "Love Is Real" does, it's prove love is real, a fact that all creatures from the endless cosmic Void absolutely despise. If a love song is powerful enough to drive these strange creatures away, who knows what it could accomplish if it was properly amplified.

You turn off the RADIO and unplug it, wrapping the chord up tight. You're taking it with you.

Glancing back over at the vents, you realizing that the manager's office might have a public announcement system through which you could play something. Of course, heading straight to the safety of the rooftop also sounds very tempting at this moment.

Crawl in rooftop vent on page 3
Crawl in manager's office vent on page 7

"Hey, is that Martha Moobin on your shirt?" you call out, climbing down from the vent and strolling over to the triceratops. "I love Martha Moobin. I've been listening to her new record like crazy."

The triceratops grins, instantly impressed. "Wait, you're a moobhead?" she questions. "Me too!"

"'Love Is Real', right? What a good song," you continue. "I've seen her four times."

The dinosaur nods excitedly. "Not bad, not bad. I'm looking at show number twelve in October."

"Whoa," you reply. "That's a real fan right there."

The triceratops lets go of the door handle and relaxes a bit, strolling back over to the machine she was working on before you stumbled in here and interrupted her.

She hesitates a moment, sizing you up one last time and then finally pushing her doubt to the side. "You're alright," she offers. "If you're a fellow moobhead then I know you're not looking for trouble."

"I'm not looking for trouble," you repeat back to her. "I just got lost and ended up back here. I'll be out of your hair in no time."

"Fair enough," the triceratops replies.

The dinosaur turns and crouches down by the machine she's working on, pulling out a wrench and diving back in.

You let out a long sigh of relief, then nonchalantly stroll back over to the door. You size up the handle, which isn't nearly as secure from this side, then kick it as hard as you can, coughing loudly as you break it off. Now there's no way for this prehistoric maintenance worker to get out until she's rescued, which will probably end up saving her life.

The dinosaur glances over at you with a face full of concern.

"Sorry, just a cough," you reply.

The triceratops nods, then gets back to work.

You creep back into the depths of the room, returning to the rooftop vent.

Crawl in rooftop vent on page 3

You approach Ben's Burger Barn with a smile on your face, taking note that the grill is still sizzling as the glorious scent of a fresh burger wafts across your nostrils.

You arrive at the counter to find a man in an apron facing away from you, his focus trained squarely on the grill in question.

He doesn't seem to notice that you're there, and normally you'd have no problem being patient but, as time ticks down, you're forced to call out to this unknown figure.

"Hey! Are you still open?" you finally shout.

The figure doesn't budge, just continues along with what he's doing. Although the sizzle from the grill is quite noisy, it shouldn't be loud enough to drown out your voice. It's possible he's ignoring you, but that doesn't make much since either.

"Hello?" you call out, making another attempt.

This seems to finally break through the man's trance, and he turns to face you, putting on a large grin as he approaches the counter. "Sorry about that, the man offers, shaking his head as though to scold himself. "I kinda drifted off there for a minute. Welcome to Ben's Burger Barn, I'm Ben."

"Nice to meet you," you reply. You're trying to focus on making your order, but you can't help but notice that Ben appears to be a little under the weather.

The man is actually quite handsome, with choppy dark hard and bright blue eyes, but there's something about these eyes that appears worn out and exhausted. He's clearly tired, working hard to maintain his composure.

You try your best to ignore it, gazing up at the menu behind him. There a few different ways of ordering your burger here at Ben's Burger Barn, mostly consisting of a side of fries and similar burger patties and with a wide variety of condiments and extra flavors heaped on top.

"I'm not entirely sure what to get," you admit. "What's the favorite?"

You glance down from the menu posted behind Ben to see that he's staring off into space once more, zoned out completely. He hasn't heard a word you've said.

"Ben," you offer, finally breaking him out of his trance for a second time. "Are you okay?"

The man smiles, but his expression falters slightly. "Yeah, it's just been a long day. Something got into the burger patties earlier and the health department's been riding my ass all day to not serve them. They threatened to shut me down! Honestly, the burgers are fine. The rodents didn't even chew them, just left some black slime on the box and went on their way."

The moment he says this another delicious waft of sizzling burger scent washes its way across your senses. It certainly doesn't *smell* like there's anything wrong with the burgers.

"I cleaned them off," Ben continues. "They're fine. You want the special? That's what Gorbo the security guard orders every day."

Decline and continue to the mall's central hub on page 52
Order one of Ben's burgers on page 17

106

As wonderful as this reality is, you've still got a little more adventure left in you. After all, it's not every day that you get a chance to go back and check out other potential timelines you happened to miss during the first run through.

Your fingers begin to dance across the keyboard.
"It's been a long day in Billings, but there's one very important stop left on your list," you recite, reading aloud as you type away feverishly. The words appear across your empty page at an incredible rate. "You're headed towards the mall in search of a gift for your son, as his 25th birthday is, technically speaking, just a few days away. No, wait. Hours away."

You realize now that, in your excitement, you've been rushing the process.

You stop typing, and suddenly the meta loop comes to a screeching halt. You hear a loud tearing sound, as though a page is being torn from a book.

You glance around and see that your desk is now sitting in a thick forest. To your right, the trees open up into a beautiful view of Lake Elmo. It's a glorious sight, but this isn't where you're supposed to be.

You take a deep breath and start over, careful not to rush things this time. You begin the opening page again.

You type the following, starting on page 1

You quickly size up the dresser and determine that you can probably take it in a fight, thanks to the baseball bat you've already acquired for your son.

You quickly pull back your weapon and take a swing at the dresser as hard as you can, knocking the sentient furniture in its side with a thunderous crack. You pull back and take another swing, but this time the dresser full of tentacles knows your attack is coming.

The bat hits a mass of the slithering appendages and becomes immediately stuck, gripped tight by the tentacles as they wrap tighter and tighter around it. The dresser is much stronger than you anticipated, and moments later the weapon is ripped from your hands.

You watch as the *BASEBALL BAT* is erupts into splinters, the tentacles completely destroying it in a matter of seconds.

The dresser keeps coming, and you now find yourself without a gift for your son.

Run around the dresser and try escaping out the back door on page 87
Attempt to push a shelf over on the monster on page 8

You can do this, you think, your eyes focused not on the swarm of horrific monsters, but on the freedom that lies beyond them. While it might be easier to turn and sprint back to the safety of the mall from which you came, that path only provides a temporary solution to this very big problem.

You ready your baseball bat and begin to duck and dodge through the snapping, hissing Void crabs. You move this way and that, weaving around the beasts as they continue to close in on you. They continue to pour out from behind the vehicles, rapidly growing in numbers, but just when it seems like the mass of monsters is too much to handle, you start swinging.

A loud crack echoes through the parking lot as your baseball bat collides with one of the abominations, splitting the enormous black crab's shell in two as it staggers back. While black tar is constantly bubbling forth from within theses monsters, it doesn't typically erupt forth like it's doing now.

The Void crab screeches and hisses, then collapses to the cement with a distinct stillness, its limbs curling toward its body and holding in place like a gnarled claw.

You take another swing at a second crab that's rushing you from behind, walloping it so hard that the create flies backwards a good ten feet, landing upside down as its hard carapace cracks down the middle and spills Voidal ooze everywhere like an enormous popping water balloon.

You keep these defensive maneuvers up for a while, but it soon becomes apparent that there are just too many of them. For every one of these horrific creatures you dispatch of, another two emerge, and soon enough you're beginning to regret your choice to push onward.

You're trapped, and no amount of swinging your bat is going to save you.

Just as it seems like all is lost, however, there's a loud roar as a security vehicle rounds the corner of the mall. You continue to fight off the Void crabs until the car pulls up next to you and pops open its door, at which point you make your escape.

You climb in and slam the door behind you, breathing a sigh of relief.

"Go!" you yell out, looking over at the familiar unicorn security guard who waits in the driver's seat.

He sits motionless, staring at you with tired, vacant eyes. The unicorn's skin had once been rosy pink, but now he's pale and sickly, and from the corner of his mouth drips a single, long streak of black liquid.

"You shouldn't be out here," the unicorn security guard finally says. "It's not safe for flesh."

"Okay," is all you can think to say, struggling to maintain your composure.

You realize now that the Void crabs surrounding this vehicle are no longer attacking it, simply waiting and watching. It's like they have a reverence for the car, or driver, and are awaiting their next command.

After staring at you for an uncomfortably long time, the unicorn security guard makes an announcement. "We should get you back inside," he says.

The unicorn turns his head forward once more, slowly driving back to the front entrance of the mall.

"We need to get out of here!" you plead. "The mall's not safe."

"Safety for the flesh, this is my duty," the unicorn security guard replies. "I have a job to do but I can't remember what it is."

You watch as the black tar that drips from the corner of his mouth becomes a constant, pouring stream. He starts to choke and sputter, but keeps his eyes on the road.

You also now notice that something has been taped to the dashboard of this vehicle, a simple notecard with a little information that might be worth remembering.

The notecard reads: air conditioning code 4711

"The open maw of time is waiting for you," the unicorn security guard states ominously as the two of you draw closer and closer to the mall.

The unicorn seems to be trapped between worlds, trying to fulfill his protective duties as a security guard while the Void melts his mind with instructions of its own. It won't be long before the endless cosmic abyss is calling all of the shots.

You begin to weigh your choices here, debating whether or not it's smarter to play along or take matters into your own hands.

Act normal and do as he says on page 79
Attack with the baseball bat on page 147

You decide that, while this ending is wonderful, there might be something even better out there. You'd love to have a gift for your son, and if this meta loop functions the way you think it does, maybe you'll be able to get him something great on the next loop around.

You flip to the first page of the book and begin to read as the world around you melts away. You watch as the walls peel back to reveal a universe passing by in reverse, the pathways of fate all curling back up onto themselves.

"It's been a long day in Billings, but there's one very important stop left on your list," you read, the words flying from your lips at an incredible rate. "You're headed towards the mall in search of a gift for your son, as his 25th birthday is, technically speaking, just hours away."

You realize now that, in your excitement, you've been rushing the story.

You stop reading, and suddenly the meta loop comes to a screeching halt. You hear a loud tearing sound, as though a page is being torn from the very book that you hold in your hands.

You glance around and see that you're standing in a thick forest. To your right, the trees open up into a beautiful view of Lake Elmo. It's a glorious sight, but this isn't where you're supposed to be.

You take a deep breath and start over, careful not to rush things this time.

You begin to read the following on page 1

The glowing lights of Brain Drain Video Games flood your eyes with sparkling neon color as you approach. Unfortunately, despite the glittering decorations and flashing signs, the place seems to be empty.

"Hello?" you call out as you cross over the threshold of the store, confirming now that it is completely vacant. "Is anyone here?"

"Hi there," comes a strange, computerized voice from all around you, causing you to jump in alarm.

You glance back and forth, struggling to determine where these vocalizations are emanating from, until finally you notice a smiling, digitally rendered face on a television screen behind the counter.

"Welcome to Brain Drain Video Games," the computer offers. "I'm Ribble, an artificial intelligence system developed by Brain Drain Industries."

"Hi Ribble," you stammer. "I'm looking for a game."

"I know," the computer replies in its digital, monotone voice. "Using proprietary algorithms based on timeline samples from across the Tingleverse, I was able to predict your arrival here, which is why the store is still open. As a highly advanced artificial intelligence, I can predict your every move with ninety-nine point nine hundred and ninety-seven percent accuracy."

You stare back at the computer, narrowing your eyes slightly as you struggle to determine whether or not this is some kind of elaborate prank.

"It's not a prank," Ribble informs you, answering your question before you even have a chance to ask it.

Your eyes go wide. "Okay, what am I thinking about right now?" you inquire, picturing something specific within your mind.

"There is an eighty-one percent chance you are thinking about a chariot made of squids that lurches forward when it they blast ink, and a nine percent chance you are thinking about a nude car," offers Ribble. "Like a car with no clothes on, just skin."

Incredible, you reply, utterly blow away by the sophistication of this computerized entity.

There's a mechanical whirring sound from somewhere behind the computer screen, this strange artificial entity processing information at an incredible rate.

"You're looking for a video game for your son," the computer announces. "I've predicted with ninety-five point four percent accuracy this is the game he will most enjoy."

A loud clang sounds and the next thing you know a small metal chute has lowered down next to you. You hear a faint sliding noise and then suddenly a video game case pops out of the chute with a hollow plastic clatter on the counter before you. The chute ascends back into the ceiling.

"Are you sure about that?" you question, picking up the game and turning it over in your hands.

"Ninety-five point four percent sure," Ribble reminds me.

Liking those odds, you reach into your pocket and pull out some cash, pushing it through a slot on the counter. Moments later, a tiny light bulb turns green and a few coins are spit back out at you for change.

"Thank you for coming," the computer calls out in its peculiar mechanical tone. "I should also say, there's a fifty-seven percent chance the number 4711 will be very important in your immediate future. Remember this code."

"Uh... what?" you stammer, not quite sure what this means.

Ribble is silent for a moment, then finally sputters out another monotone "thank you for coming."

You turn and stroll back out the way you arrived, VIDEO GAME in hand. It's time to head home.

Head back to the front doors on page 83

You grab ahold of the green tarp and quickly wrap it around the end of your metal pole, then hoist this creation up into the air. You wave it frantically back and forth, doing everything you can to attract the attention of the helicopter above.

At first it seems hopeless, as their focus remains on sending bolts of magically concentrated love down into the swarming Void creatures. Eventually, however, you spot one of the wizards pointing in your direction, yelling out to someone else in the vehicle who's wearing a dark Anti-Voidal Task Force uniform.

The two of them exchange quite a few words, continuing to point at you while you jump up and down with excitement.

The man in the uniform pulls out a set of binoculars and places them over his eyes for a better look. He stays like this for a good while and then suddenly pulls them away, shaking his head.

The helicopter begins to swoop in a different direction, taking another pass at raining down some magical eruptions on the swarms below.

"Wait!" you cry out desperately. "Come back! I need help!"

They're too far away to hear you, obviously, and even if you were up close you likely wouldn't be audible over the roaring blades.

Suddenly, another sound enters your ears, this one much more frightening than the hum of a helicopter.

You turn around to see that several winged Void crabs have scuttled over the edge of the rooftop. They have you in their sights and immediately begin to flutter in your direction with their teeth bared and their pinchers snapping.

The monsters are just too quick for you to react. You try your best to fight them off with the metal pole but one of them grabs ahold of your wrist with it's powerful pincher. The makeshift weapon falls from your hand, clattering to the ground. You let out a frantic scream and tumble over as more and more of the creatures make their way over the edge of the building.

The Void crabs begin to bite, pinch and tear, completely covering you in a ravenous mass.

THE END

As you sprint towards Fashion Forward you see that it has been left halfway shuttered, and the space between the metallic rolling cage and the floor is more than enough for you to slide through.

"Become me!" the monster behind you bellows, gnashing its teeth and snapping the air with its mighty pinchers.

The creature is close on your heels, but not quite fast enough to catch up with you as you push forth one final burst of speed. With all the energy you can muster, you drop to the smooth tile floor of the mall, sliding under the metal cage and immediately spinning around to grip it with your hands on the other side. You throw down the rolling security feature as hard as you can, then jump in alarm as monster who was once a unicorn security guard slams against the metal with a deafening rattle.

The creature hisses and screeches, reaching out for you with its tentacles and claws through the slits in the cage. However, the beast is much to large to get through, and not quite strong enough to break the whole thing down.

You watch in awe as the monster continues to push against the metal, however, and soon enough you find yourself lost in a trance, gazing past the gaping maw of this beast and into the infinite cosmos beyond.

"Yes, feast upon the knowledge. Understand the beginning and the end. Understand your decay," the creature moans in the voice of a thousand collapsing stars.

You can feel your mind flooding with information that no mortal should ever attempt to understand, and the sensation is intoxicating. Somehow, though, you know to pull away.

With every bit of discipline you can muster, you tear your gaze away from the beast, shutting your eyes tight and thinking of anything else.

You picture cute bigfeet playing tennis on a sunny day. You picture a handsome tree waving to you in the front yard. You picture the wonderful taste of the upcoming cake at your son's birthday.

Eventually, the squeals and hisses dissipate. The monster pulls away from the metal grate, disappointed that its prey has won this round. It stumbles off in the direction from which it came, a bubbling mess of mouths, tentacles, eyes, limbs and claws.

Soon enough, you find yourself alone in the store, or so it seems.

You stand up and brush yourself off, getting a feel for your surroundings. The shop is a complete mess, with clothing scattered everywhere and shelves toppled over like shattered furniture skeletons.

The lights are dim, but at the back of the store you can see a door that presumably leads to the outer concourse of the mall. Hopefully, freedom comes shortly thereafter.

You creep deeper into the store, your eyes focused and your senses on high alert.

Without warning, a nearby dresser springs to life, revealing itself to be a sentient object as it rushes toward you. The drawers erupt open as it rumbles forward, dozens of long, black tentacles bursting forth from within.

Run around the dresser and try escaping out the back door on page 87
Attempt to push a shelf over on the monster on page 8
Attack the monster with your baseball bat (if you have one one) on page 107

You grab the microphone and pull it toward you, then let loose with a barrage of insults that carry out over the mall's public announcement system. Your voice booms through the entire building, echoing down every corridor and through the aisles of each store.

"Get out of here!" you cry out. "No Void allowed! We don't want you!"

The swarming mass of creatures begins to move and undulate, your words whipping them into a frenzy. You're not sure if this is a good or bad thing, so you just keep going.

"Go back to your own timeline!" you shout. "Oops, I forgot. You don't have one! You come from nothingness!"

The creatures begin to shriek and squeal, driven mad with anger and aggression.

Unfortunately, it only takes one glimpse of you up in the manager's office for the whole slew of them to start tumbling in your direction. The swarm begins to heave toward you, climbing up on top of one another as they stretch out and attempt to reach the booth.

"Looks like there's not enough of you to get me!" you call out with a laugh.

Suddenly, your words catch in your throat. From the fray, you begin to see a handful of the creatures taking flight, somehow mutated to sprout insect-like wings upon their back. The Void crabs aren't terribly good at flying, but that doesn't seem to matter as the careen towards the glass of your second story office.

There is a loud crack as one of the Void crabs slams into the window, then another and another. You stumble back, dropping the microphone as your eyes widen in a state of utter terror.

You turn around, hoping to climb back into the vent, but before you can hoist yourself up you hear a loud crash behind you as the monsters burst through, sending shards everywhere. The flying Void crabs instantly lunge toward you, snapping their claws and hissing loudly.

You feel sharp daggers of pain course through your body as the creatures grab you and pull you back, and the next thing you know the hungry beasts are all over you. You cry out for help, but you already know that it's much too late for that.

The creatures overwhelm you and begin their feast.

THE END

118

"And the wizards started blasting magic love beams at the crabs?" your son's friend, Heather, questions. "Out of freaking *helicopters?*"

You nod. "They saved my life."

It's your son's birthday, but right now all the attention is on you. Your son's friends have packed the dining room, where you sit on a chair in the middle of the crowd and field questions about your wild night at the Billings Mall. Everyone had been following on the news, locked down in their homes while your adventure unfolded in the heart of the action.

They want to know all the details, and you're happy to give them up, so long as it doesn't take away from the real reason you're all gathered here today. Fortunately, your son seems just as interested as everyone else does.

"Did you actually see the security guard change?" Pete, another one of your son's friends questions. "You saw him grow claws and tentacles and stuff?"

"He was chasing me through the mall when it happened," you offer. "I saw that whole thing."

The crowd gasps.

"I'm lucky I made it out alive," you continue.

Now it's time for your son to step up. He places his hand lovingly on your shoulder. "Luck had nothing to do with it. You had a lot of important choices to make along the way and look where that brought you."

You smile. "Well, I'm happy to be alive, but my life isn't the one we're celebrating today," you blurt, changing the subject. "My son is one year older and one year wiser!"

Everyone applauds, hooting and hollering as your son smiles.

"Let's get the gifts started," someone calls out from the crowd.

"You go first," Heather chimes in, nodding in your direction.

If you don't have a gift turn to page 123
If you don't have a gift, but you found the red flag, turn to page 88
If you got him a baseball bat turn to page 126
If you got him a video game turn to page 145
If you got him a necktie turn to page 127
If you got him a book turn to page 128

You turn the radio dial to the local news, curious about what's going on in the outside world. Immediately, a confident song comes thundering out over the speakers, flooding the room with a familiar theme for breaking stories.

"Cref Bobbins here for Billings Action News," the reporter begins. "It seems the timeline tear at Lake Elmo was just the beginning of a frightening day here in Billings. While authorities had hoped this rift in potential realities was allowing temporary access to a nearby, similar timeline, it turns out the tear went much deeper than expected. We have received official word that the endless cosmic Void is currently leaking into Billings, and all citizens have been recommended to follow Void Encounter Emergency Protocol. This means staying inside and turning of your lights, as well as barricading all doors and windows. It's recommended that citizens refrain for gazing into The Void itself, or even thinking too critically about the nature of The Void, as this could cause Void Madness."

Your anxiety grows as you hear the news, overwhelmed by just how bad it has gotten out there. At least this means the authorities know there's a problem and are working to stop it.

"The Billings Police have handed over this developing situation to the Montana Anti-Voidal Task Force. Some of their helicopters have already arrived in Billings, and they are using highly trained Montanan wizards to disperse the Voidal creatures who have entered this timeline. In addition, they have this message for anyone who may still be stranded outside of their own home:"

A song begins to softly play over the radio, not enough to obscure the words, but enough to provide a pleasant background for the messages they're about to deliver. You notice the tentacles that have grown off the half-eaten burger next to you twitch slightly.

"The Anti-Voidal Task Force has asked me to relay this message," Cref Bobbins continues. "While this loving music plays, Voidal creatures, or those who have been infected by The Void, will not listen. This allows for the delivery of important information to citizens who are still within the containment zone. Anyone who can still hear this message should wave a red or blue flag to alert the helicopters. Any other flag color with be ignored, as those waving them may actually be creatures of The Void."

The second you hear this message your gaze falls upon a red Billings Mustangs jersey hanging in the locker nearby. You stand up and walk over to it. There are a few rips and tears in the fabric, so it might not function too well as a sports uniform any longer, but it would make a perfect RED FLAG.

You take the shirt with you.

Turn off the radio on page 101
Change the channel to The Top Pop Hits with Brindle Creems on page 102
Crawl into the rooftop vent on page 3
Crawl into the manager's office vent on page 7

You take the radio that you found in the security guard's office and place it directly before the public announcement microphone. As much as you'd enjoy letting loose on these creeping, crawling Voidal creatures with an angry diatribe, you've got an idea that you think might be much more effective.

You flip on the radio and turn it up, smiling wide as an endless programming block of "Love Is Real" by Martha Moobin erupts from the speakers. You reach over and hold down a button on the microphone, and soon enough the passionate vocals of Martha Moobin are cascading out across the entire mall.

"Love is real! Love is true! From buckaroo to buckaroo!" she belts out at the top of her lungs, repeating this chorus over and over again.

The creeping, crawling beasts of the food court immediately react, whipped into a frenzy by this expression of love. They begin to squeal and shriek, trembling wildly as they tumble in circles and lash out at the air above them with wild claws. Seconds later, they start to burst, seizing up and erupting in puffs of ash that drifts off into the nothingness from which they came.

It's working, you realize, it's really working.

Suddenly, however, you notice a frightening sight making its way towards you through the food court. Galloping across the crowd is the enormous, horrifying creature that was once a unicorn security guard. You'd thought you were safe positioned up here on the second floor, gazing out across the food court below, but this former security guard is now tall enough to bust through the window and swallow you whole.

Closer and closer the creature lumbers, the Void crabs collapsing all around it but its gargantuan form seemingly unaffected.

The monster lets out a terrifying roar that rattles the glass between you, preparing to leap and then suddenly stopping in its tracks. The beast stumbles a bit, trying to regain its footing and then faltering even more. You watch as his mutated form begins to crack and crumble, transforming into ash piece by piece until finally he dissolves into nothing more than a wispy pile of dust.

You keep the radio going, but once ample time has passed you open up the door next to you and take some stairs down into the food court. A layer of dark grey ash covers everything, but there are no longer any signs of The Void to be found.

"Hey!" comes a stern and powerful voice.

You turn to see four wizards flanked by a team in Anti-Voidal Task Force uniforms. They rush into the food court on high alert, securing the premises.

"What happened?" one of the wizard asks as they approach you.

"Looks like they weren't into the new Martha Moobin track," you reply.

You turn and head out toward the parking lot. It's late, and you've got a birthday to attend in the afternoon.

Get some rest and head to your son's birthday on page 77

Your expression falters slightly, but you quickly pull yourself together and straighten up. There's no reason to bring down the atmosphere of your son's party just because you couldn't manage to retrieve a gift for him.

"I actually... don't have a present this time," you stammer. "I'm sorry, buddy."

Your son smiles. He doesn't seem disappointed in the least. "That's okay, you had a big night. I'm just thankful you're alive after all that. The last thing you need to worry about is getting me a birthday present."

"It feels strange taking a trip to the mall and going through all that to end up with nothing," you reply.

"*The Void* is nothing," your son replies wisely. "You know that first hand. What's happening right now is... everything else."

You look around at all the smiling friends and family, quickly realizing your son is right. This is what matters. It would've been great to find him that perfect gift, but there are plenty of birthdays to come.

You hug your son. "I love you," you offer.

"I love you, too," he replies. "Thanks for making it back in one piece."

THE END

You take the red Billings Mustangs unicorn you're carrying with you and quickly wrap it around the end of your metal pole, then hoist this creation up into the air. You wave it frantically back and forth, doing everything you can to attract the attention of the helicopter above.

At first it seems hopeless, as their focus remains on sending bolts of magically concentrated love down into the swarming Void creatures. Eventually, however, you spot one of the wizards pointing in your direction, yelling out to someone else in the vehicle who's wearing a dark Anti-Voidal Task Force uniform.

The two of them exchange quite a few words, continuing to point at you while you jump up and down with excitement.

The man in the uniform pulls out a set of binoculars and places them over his eyes for a better look. He stays like this for a good while and then suddenly pulls them away, nodding his head in confirmation.

The helicopter immediately alters course, swooping around and taking a direct route to your location on the roof. You watch as a ladder is tossed from the side of the vehicle, snaking down towards you as the air begins to rush past.

The blades are loud and unnerving, but soon another sound enters your ears, this one much more frightening than the hum of a helicopter.

You turn around to see that several winged Void crabs have scuttled over the edge of the rooftop. They have you in their sights and immediately begin to flutter in your direction with their teeth bared and their pinchers snapping.

With seconds to spare, the first rung of the ladder finally reaches your hand, and you grab onto it tightly as the helicopter begins to lift off.

Your feet leave the ground, but these creatures are just as capable of flight as you are. One of the Void crabs lunges at you, its claws extended, but just before he gets a chance to grip your flesh a bolt of magical energy flies past you and smashes into the monster. The Void crab is blown apart, his Voidal energy disintegrating and drifting away like ash in the wind.

Two more blasts of magic shoot past you from the wizard above, taking out another pair of Void crabs that are hot on your trail. Soon enough, the monsters are no longer following.

You gaze down at The Billings Mall as you float away, watching as the Anti-Voidal Task Force continues to close in.

You're exhausted, and you've got a big day tomorrow.

Get some rest and head to your son's birthday on page 118

You reach over and grab an oblong box from the table of wrapped gifts, handing it to your son.

"Here you go," you offer.

Your son smiles and begins to unwrap. When he finally realizes what it is he seems genuinely pleased, pulling out the wooden baseball bat and holding it up for the rest of his friends to see.

"This is awesome," your son gushes, then gives you a big hug. "Thank you so much."

Your son glances over at his friend Pete, who is also a member of his local recreational team.

"What do you think?" your son asks. "Pick up game at the park after cake?"

You're sitting on a green grassy knoll as your son and his friends play ball on the field before you. Everyone is having a great time, the atmosphere casual and full of laughter.

You find yourself overwhelmed with feelings of gratitude. Even after all that chaos and destruction, the world is still turning. Despite a timeline tear into The Void threatening to destroy all of Billings, people are still here in the park playing baseball.

Your son yells over to you, his voice cutting through your thoughts. "Hey! You wanna take a swing?"

You'd normally decline, but your recent adventure has put a spring in your step. "I'm in!" you call out, jumping to your feet and running over to join them.

THE END

You reach over and grab one of the wrapped packages nearby, handing it to your son.

He opens it up, revealing a small box with a label that says "Fashion Forward". Your son smiles when he sees it, recognizing the brand immediately. He's knows what's coming next.

"Aw, thank you," he gushes as he reveals the tie you picked out for him. Your son holds out the strip of fabric for everyone to see, eliciting a series of compliments from the crowd.

"That's gonna look great with your new suit," his friend Heather says.

Your son nods, then hesitates. He's pondering something.

"Is everything okay?" you question.

Your son smiles. "Yeah, I was just thinking... I know you've been asking about coming into work with me for some time and I always tell you it's not a good day. How'd you like to come in with me tomorrow?"

You're incredibly touched by this gesture, nodding in acceptance as you struggle to find the words.

"That would be great," you finally reply, holding back tears. "That would be great."

"I'm sure everyone at the office is gonna have a lot of questions about your big adventure," he tells you.

"Sounds like a lot of fun," you reply. "I can't wait."

THE END

You smile knowingly, then hand your son a small, wrapped gift from a nearby assortment of boxes.

He thanks you and tears away the paper, gradually revealing a book hidden within. He reads the title and laughs. "This is crazy!" he offers, showing the paperback to his crowd of friends and then turning his attention back to you. "Escape From The Billings Mall? How did you find this?"

"I got a pretty solid recommendation about it," you inform him.

"Is it about... what happened yesterday?" he questions, a little confused. "That's Chuck Tingle level turnaround time."

"I don't know," you explain. "I'm not supposed to read it or I'll create a timeline loop. I had to promise."

Your son laughs, flashing you an odd look but still very pleased with his gift. He thanks you again and gives you a strong hug, then moves on the the rest of his presents.

"I guess that's why hand removal is so important," Snow Channel Pete says to you from the static of the television screen, closing out his news segment. "Back to you, Weatherman."

You're lying on the living room couch as light from the television static dances across the dark room around you. You'd think you would instantly fall asleep after such a big adventure the night before, but instead you find yourself unable to slow down. A little bit of Snow Channel has managed to soothe you, but you're still not ready to hit they hay just yet.

You sense a presence behind you and sit up, then relax when you see it's just your son coming down the stairs.

"Hey," he offers, then sits down on the couch next to you. "I flipped through the book you got me. I can see why you were worried about reading it."

You nod. "I trust the person who recommended it."

"It was really good," your son continues. "I'm so proud of you. I mean, I already was, but now that I understand what really happened at the mall... you did a great job."

"Thank you," you reply, accepting his praise.

"There is one thing, though," your son explains. "You got away, but there's a timeline where you stopped The Void *yourself*, without running.

I want you to know that I really like this ending but... if you want to go back and try it again, I understand."

"Really?" you question. The thought hadn't even crossed your mind.

You son hands you the book. "Just be careful. I want to see you at my birthday party on every timeline, not just this one."

With that, he stands up and heads up the stairs. "I'm proud of you either way," your son calls back over his shoulder.

Eventually, it's just you sitting alone with the book in your hands. The only sound is the static hum of The Snow Channel.

If you're happy with this ending, turn to page 142
If you want to go back, turn to page 92

You reach over and grab an oblong box from the table full of gifts, handing it to your son.

"Here you go," you offer.

Your son smiles and begins to unwrap. When he finally realizes what it is he seems genuinely pleased, pulling out the wooden bat and holding it up for the rest of his friends to see.

"This is awesome," your son gushes, then gives you a big hug. "Thank you so much. After the party let's go to the batting cages and try it out."

You watch as the machine whirs to life, then erupts with a single baseball traveling at incredible speed toward your son.

His reflexes are quick. He swings hard, putting everything he's got into the movement as a loud crack rings out. The baseball flies back and hits the metal cage with a loud rattle.

The balls start blasting out at a steady pace and you watch with pride as your son has no problem taking down each and every one of them.

When your son is finally finished, he steps out of the batting cage to meet you. "You wanna take another spin?" he questions.

You shake your head. "No thanks, my hands are a little sore."

"Well, that was really fun," your son continues.

Suddenly, a mother and daughter approach you. "I'm so sorry," the woman says. "I don't normally do this but, we saw you on the news. It's amazing the way you battled those Void crabs like that."

"Oh, thanks," you stammer, completely taken off guard.

"Could we get a picture?" the woman continues.

"Of course!" you reply.

They step up next to you and your son takes the woman's phone, strolling to the other side of the room and preparing to take a photo. "Alright everyone," he starts. "One, two, three. Smile!"

Your son snaps a few shots.

Your focus right now isn't on the camera itself, but on your son behind it. He's wearing an expression that moves you to your core. In this moment, he couldn't be more thrilled that you've been recognized after your adventure.

You've spent so much time being proud of him that you didn't realizing the touching reality that right now: he's proud of you.

THE END

You approach Books For Buds to find that, to your relief, the store is still open. Unfortunately, with every step forward your walk begins to stagger even more, your feet literally dragging across the ground now.

A scaly green raptor stands at the store entrance waiting for you, long blonde hair rolling down around her shoulders. It appears the dinosaur was expecting you, and she wears a look of solemn disappointment across her face. She forces a smile as you finally reach her.

"Rough day?" she questions.

"Do I know you?" you blurt, but the last word is cut off by a spastic cough.

The beautiful green raptor steps back a bit as black ooze erupts out from between your lips in a wet, spit-take cloud. You reach up and touch the corner of you mouth, pulling your fingers away to see that they're dotted with a thick, glistening tar.

"Oh shit," you stammer. "What's happening to me?"

"I'm gonna be honest, you've done a terrible job so far," the dinosaur informs you, walking around the storefront desk and grabbing some tissues. She hands a generous helping of the soft paper to you with her clawed hand as she continues. "You've been exposed to The Void. There's not much time."

"Not much time until what?" you question, wiping the black liquid from your lips.

"Best case scenario, you transform into a horrific beast of the endless cosmic abyss. Worst case scenario, the tiny void crabs growing inside you simply burst out of your stomach and eat you alive," the blonde raptor explains, "and all kinds of other horrific options lie somewhere in between."

The strange chanting within your mind has grown into a deafening pulse, thundering through your brain as your body begins to tremble and shake. You can feel a stream of cold liquid pouring out of your nose now, and another running down the side of your neck as it bubbles up from deep within your ear.

"What do I do?" you stammer.

"You create a meta loop," the prehistoric bookseller explains. She hands you a paperback.

You look down to find the title *Escape From The Billings Mall* looking back up to you. The building on the cover appears inexplicably like the one that you're currently standing in.

As you stare, a few drops of black tar splatter across the image, slipping out from somewhere behind your face.

"You're a character in this book," the raptor explains. "That's how I knew you'd show up on these particular pages in such bad shape. The good news is, if you start to read then the loop will begin again."

"I don't understand," you stammer, your voice bubbly and strange as the liquid fills your mouth. You can feel a strange tickling sensation deep within the pit of your stomach now.

"You'll see," the raptor offers, tapping the paperback's cover with her long, sharp claw. "Why don't you read the first page aloud."

Without hesitation, you open up to the first line of *Escape From The Billings Mall*, clearing as much Voidal ooze from your throat as possible. You begin to read.

Start the book on page 1

You reach over and grab one of the wrapped packages nearby, handing it to your son.

He opens it up, revealing a small box with a label that says "Fashion Forward". Your son smiles when he sees it, recognizing the brand immediately. He's knows what's coming next.

"Aw, thank you," he gushes as he reveals the tie you picked out for him. Your son holds out the strip of fabric for everyone to see, eliciting a series of compliments from the crowd.

"Hey! Look outside!" one of the other party-goers suddenly calls out.

The group exchanges confused glances before standing up and heading to the living room windows, gazing out to see that the front yard is packed full of reporters.

"What's going on?" you stammer. "Why are they here?"

Your son laughs. "They're here for you. You're the hero today, remember?"

The thought hadn't even crossed your mind, but now that you realize what's going on you're actually kind of excited.

"Do you wanna talk to them?" your son asks.

You consider this for a moment, then nod. "Sounds fun to be on the news," you reply, "but you've gotta be there with me."

Your son laughs, then begins to loop his new tie around his neck. He tightens up the knot, looking sharp as ever.

"Ready," he finally says, then opens up the door for you to head out and meet the excited crowd.

You walk down the front steps as the reporters all converge upon you, holding out their microphones as the cameras roll. You begin to field their questions, and as you glance over you see that your son is right there with you. He's smiling wide, proud as can be, and his new tie looks great.

THE END

You smile knowingly, then hand your son a small, wrapped gift from a nearby assortment of boxes.

He thanks you and tears away the paper, gradually revealing a book hidden within. He reads the title and laughs. "This is crazy!" he offers, showing the paperback to his crowd of friends and then turning his attention back to you. "Escape From The Billings Mall? How did you find this?"

"I got a pretty solid recommendation about it," you inform him.

"Is it about... what happened yesterday?" he questions, a little confused. "That's Chuck Tingle level turnaround time."

"I don't know," you explain. "I'm not supposed to read it or I'll create a timeline loop. I had to promise."

Your son laughs, flashing you an odd look but still very pleased with his gift. He thanks you again and gives you a strong hug, then moves on the the rest of his presents.

"I guess that's why hand removal is so important," Snow Channel Pete says to you from the static of the television screen, closing out his news segment. "Back to you, Weatherman."

You're lying on the living room couch as light from the television static dances across the dark room around you. You'd think you would instantly fall asleep after such a big adventure the night before, but instead you find yourself unable to slow down. A little bit of Snow Channel has managed to soothe you, but you're still not ready to hit they hay just yet.

You sense a presence behind you and sit up, then relax when you see it's just your son coming down the stairs.

"Hey," he offers, then sits down on the couch next to you. "I flipped through the book you got me. I can see why you were worried about reading it."

You nod. "I trust the person who recommended it."

"It was really good," your son continues. "I'm so proud of you. I mean, I already was, but now I understand what *really* happened at the mall. You did a great job. I figured you might be curious, so I wanted to come down and let you know that this is one of the best endings you could've hoped for," your son explains."

"Oh, really?" you reply, eyes wide.

Your son nods. "It was fun to read. In fact, *you* should think about writing a select your own timeline story. I think you could come up with something really great."

The second that he says this, something clicks within you. It's a great idea.

"Don't stay up too late," your son offers, finally standing and nodding goodnight. He turns and heads back upstairs, into the darkness of the house.

You sit for a few more minutes as the Snow Channel continues to buzz, then turn it off. You've got too many ideas floating around within your head now. You can't wait any longer.

Abruptly, you climb to your feet, marching upstairs to your room. Once inside, you immediately head to your desk and sit down, opening up your laptop.

You open a fresh document on your word processor, then start with the title, Escape From The Billings Mall. You noticed that the book you gave your son didn't have an author listed, and maybe there's a reason for that. Maybe the author is you.

As you prepare to enter your first words, you can feel the layers of meta reality starting to collapse around you, the walls stretching and distorting with every press of the keyboard. You freeze, both excited and scared, debating whether or not you want to continue this adventure for adventure's sake.

Maybe you should change the title, avoiding the inevitable creation of a timeline loop.

Change the title on page 141
Keep the title on page 106

As the hissing, snapping creatures close in, you realize that the only safe way out of this is to turn and head back to the mall.

Without hesitation, you spin on your heels and break out in a mad dash toward the building, weaving around what cars there are left as the swarm closes in behind you. These crustaceans are incredibly fast, but you refuse to look back to get a read on their position. Instead, you keep your gaze focused directly on the broken glass window from which you emerged.

Your heart slams hard within your chest as your feet hit the pavement, transforming from a dull thud to a distinct crunch as you make your way over the shattered glass.

The second you make it back inside, you spin around and grab one of the nearby food court tables. It's twice as heavy as you'd expect, which is both good and bad given the circumstances. While you have a hell of a time dragging it over to the opening, you know that once it's in position you'll have plenty of time to figure out what's next.

You begin to lift the table, groaning loudly as your muscles strain. You're giving it everything that you've got, pushing with all your might as the swarm screeches and gargles, just seconds away from overwhelming you.

Fortunately, you manage to close the gap just in time, the table tipping forward just enough to keep it propped against the opening you've created.

There are small spaces in between that the Void crabs reach their pinchers through, snapping their claws frantically in the air, but the beasts are too large make it through otherwise, especially with their hard, wide shells to contend with.

The creatures begin to spread out a bit, tapping on the glass that covers the entire food court wall as they test their options. It seems to be holding them at bay for now, but as you watch you can see more of these horrific abominations emerging from the distant forest, rushing over to join their friends.

You can tell just from watching them that the crabs are not particularly smart, and figure their desire to get inside might be driven entirely by a hunter's instinct. They don't know that the mall is empty, they're just looking for food.

Of course, there' still at least one unfortunate soul left inside the building. Lucky you.

138

Now that your car is no longer an option, and the food court won't remain safe for very long, you decide to head back to the mall's central hub and look for another way out.

Return to the central hub and look for another way out on page 143

Your expression falters slightly, but you quickly pull yourself together and straighten up. There's no reason to bring down the atmosphere of your son's party just because you couldn't manage to retrieve a gift for him.

"I actually... don't have a present this time," you stammer. "I'm sorry, buddy."

Your son smiles. He doesn't seem disappointed in the least. "That's okay, you had a big night. I'm just thankful you're alive after all that. The last thing you need to worry about is getting me a birthday present."

"It feels strange taking a trip to the mall and going through all that to end up with nothing," you reply.

"*The Void* is nothing," your son replies wisely. "You know that first hand. What's happening right now is... everything else."

You look around at all the smiling friends and family, quickly realizing your son is right. This is what matters. It would've been great to find him that perfect gift, but there are plenty of birthdays to come.

You hug your son. "I love you," you offer.

"I love you, too," he replies. "Thanks for making it back in one piece."

After an hour or so of reveling, Heather finds you and pulls you to the side. The two of you duck into the living room while the rest of the party enjoys their cake and ice cream.

"You know, I was at the mall yesterday, too," Heather informs you.

"Really?" you question, your eyes going wide. "I'm so glad you made it out okay."

Your son's friend shakes her head. "No, no. I was there much earlier in the afternoon. The timeline tear hadn't even happened yet," she explains. "Something really strange *did* happen, though."

Heather reaches into her bag and pulls out a book, handing it to you. You read the cover, which is emblazoned with the words, "Escape From The Billings Mall."

"I was looking for a present for your son at the bookstore," she explains. "There was a dinosaur working there and she approached me with this book. She said I should give it to you."

"Me?" you question, confused.

140

"Yeah," Heather continues. "The raptor offered it up for free, so I took it. Now it's yours."

Heather hands you to book, then hears someone calling out for her in the other room. She smiles and leaves, allowing you a moment on your own to look over this bizarre paperback.

You crack open the book and find that there's a note tucked inside from the dinosaur at the book store.

"Dear reader," you recite aloud. "I took a peek at the last few pages, or middle pages that end the story, technically speaking. It really is the thought that counts, but in case you were curious, this book is your ticket to another meta layer of reality. There are other paths where you showed up with a gift, and if you think it's worth it, you can ride a meta loop back to them. Reading the book you hold in your hands will put you right where this all started. You might make things a little better, but they could also get much, much worse. The choice is yours, but be careful."

You consider this offer, the meta layers of reality beginning to tremble and vibrate around you in anticipation.

If you're happy with this ending turn to page 142
Open the book on page 110

Your son's words begin to repeat over and over again in your heard, a stern warning and a prayer for gratitude. He told you this is one of the best endings you could've hoped for, and you should listen.

You let out a long sigh and press backspace a few times as the walls stop shaking.

You begin to type out the title again, reciting the words as you go.

"Escape From The *Bozeman* Mall," you announce proudly. "Page one."

THE END

142

You decide that, as exciting as it sounds to travel between timelines as you hunt for the best possible result to your journey, once is enough.

After all, that's probably what caused this timeline tear to happen in the first place.

You place Escape From The Billings Mall on a nearby shelf in the living room. Maybe you'll open it up and take it for a spin some other time, but right now you're more than happy with the hand that fate has dealt.

THE END

Your pace doubled and your senses on high alert, you begin the trek back toward the heart of the mall. Once you reach the central hub, you'll be able to branch out into the various sections and, hopefully, find another way out.

You don't get far before your notice footsteps lumbering behind you, however. You glance back over your shoulder to see that, several yards back, the unicorn security guard is following. By now is face is absolutely covered with Voidal ooze, pouring out of him and leaving a long, toxic path of splatters across the floor behind. The security guard is staggering as he moves, dragging his feet as his body begins to contort and change.

"You're not supposed to be here after hours!" the unicorn calls out, his strange gurgling voice echoing through the hallway. "Hours turn into days, days turn into weeks, weeks turn into millennia. The infinite moan of space is here already!"

The entity behind you continues to rant and rave as you break out in a full-on spirt, hoping to put as much space between you and the security guard as possible. You take one final glance back over your shoulder to see that he's almost completely unrecognizable now, shifting even more by the second.

Enormous, crablike appendages have erupted from the creature's back, and he's now using these to scuttle along behind you. His head has opened up into two distinct halves from which several black tentacles have erupted in a squealing, lashing mass. He is no longer a being of this world, but a creature from the depths of the endless cosmic Void.

"No running in the mall!" the security monster screams, his voice bizarre and strangled, as though a hundred different creatures are calling out the words in unison from across the galaxy.

You're running as fast as you can now, and the creature is thundering along right behind. You can see the central hub approaching fast, and quickly make your decision about which direction to head. As far as you know, there are only four stores that might still offer an escape.

Head to Books For Buds on page 11
Head to Fashion Forward on page 114
Head to Brain Drain Video Games on page 67
Head to The Sport Spot on page 59

You can do this, you think, your eyes focused not on the swarm of horrific monsters, but on the freedom that lies beyond them. While it might be easier to turn and sprint back to the safety of the mall from which you came, that path only provides a temporary solution to this very big problem.

You begin to duck and dodge through the snapping, hissing Void crabs. You move this way and that, weaving around the beasts as they rapidly close in on you. They continue to pour out from behind the vehicles, growing in numbers, and soon enough you begin to rethink your decision.

There's a lot more of these strange creatures than you originally thought, and they don't seem to be stopping.

You glance back over your shoulder at the mall entrance, hoping there still might be a path to safety should you change your mind and alter course. Unfortunately, the Void crabs have already blocked any chance of escape in this direction.

You realize now that you're trapped, not a single route left that isn't completely covered by these swarming, gurgling crustaceans from the endless cosmic abyss.

Maybe if you took a running leap you could barely make it over the crabs to your left, you think, but before you have a chance to enact this plan you feel a sharp pain in your ankle.

You stumble forward onto the cement, trying everything you can manage to stay upright but realizing now that your foot is refusing to obey. Glancing back reveals an enormous Void crab with his pincher crushing your foot, regardless of how furiously you struggle to kick him off.

Within seconds the rest of the creatures are upon you, spitting up their toxic Voidal tar as they screeching and snap excitedly. They cover you in a hungry, swarming mass, tearing you apart.

THE END

You reach over and grab one of the wrapped packages nearby, handing it to your son.

He grins wide, immediately recognizing the size and shape of this gift as something he's been receiving over the course of several holidays since childhood.

You son tears off the colorful wrapping paper to reveal exactly what he though, a brand new video game.

"Sweet!" he gushes, showing the rest of his friends who all nod approvingly.

"Did you pick this out?" he questions, impressed by your selection.

"The store helped," you offer in return.

"Someone at the store?" your son repeats back to you, trying to understand what exactly you're saying.

"No, the actual store," you explain, but he still doesn't quite get it.

Instead, your son shrugs and thanks you with a powerful hug.

Over the next few minutes, the gifts are opened one by one. Still, everyone's eyes seem to be locked on the new video game, and once every bit of wrapping paper has been torn the party heads into your living room to check it out.

"You wanna do the honors?" your son questions, handing you the game.

You nod, walking over to the television and turning it on. Before you have a change to do anything else, however, a blast of static fills your vision. Typically, it takes you a while for you to settle in and receive transmissions from The Snow Channel, but today it's instant.

You gaze at the static in a trance as the host, Snow Channel Pete, appears. He's thin and gaunt, with pale skin and a pin-striped suit.

"Breaking news: the layers have been closed," Snow Channel Pete reveals, speaking directly to you. "Someone was moving too fast between timelines and caused a tear in the way things are, connecting it to the way things were and the way things could be. Problem is, that's very close to the way things *can never be.*"

"I understand," you tell him in a monotone drone.

"You did a good job," Snow Channel Pete informs you. "Not many buckaroos could handle a situation like that and come out the other side with their skin on tight."

"Thanks," you offer.

"No, thank you," Snow Channel Pete continues. "You keep The Void out of *your timeline*. I'll keep it out of mine."

Suddenly, the loading screen of the new video game appears before you, instantly snapping you out of your trance. Snow Channel Pete is gone, and your son's friends are all staring at you awkwardly.

"Sorry about that," you announce, standing up again.

You grab a controller off the nearby coffee table. "Who wants to go first?"

THE END

Sure, the unicorn security guard is keeping you safe for now, but his evolution into a creature of the endless cosmic Void is not slowing down. Who knows what might happen the next time you encounter him.

Besides, if you can commandeer his vehicle right here and now, your path to freedom is quick and simple. With this security guard out of the way, all you have to do is climb into the driver's seat and step on the gas.

You grip the bat tightly in your hands, struggling to determine the best method of attack. There's not nearly enough room for a full on swing, but you can probably strike him with the hard end like a stabbing lance.

Your heart slamming within your chest, you brace yourself for the sudden outburst to come, preparing your mind and body for the battle ahead. It feels like the world is moving in slow motion.

Until it's not.

You snap the baseball bat forward, striking the unicorn security guard in the head and knocking him against the window. He seems surprised, but terrifyingly unfazed, as though his body has become immune to pain during its transformation.

The car stops and he snaps his head toward you, eyes inhumanly wide and mouth agape as black tar bubbles forth in a cascade of sickening liquid. He lets out a high pitched screech unlike anything you've ever heard, and his body begins to shift and transform, mutating before your very eyes in heaving, throbbing mass.

The unicorn's mouth opens wider and wider still, unhinging at the jaw with a disturbing pop as a mass of lashing tentacles erupt forth, along with a several enormous, insect-like appendages.

These tentacles grip the bat in your hands, pulling it from your grasp and yanking it into the dark abyss of its throat. You let out a scream as the creature grows larger and larger, filling the entire space of the car and pulling you into its own chaotic mass.

THE END

As you approach Ben's Burger Barn you immediately notice that something is wrong. Smoke is pouring upward from the grill behind the front counter where the charred remains of a burnt, extra crispy burger sit blackened and destroyed. The smell is terrible, and you're quite surprised the fire alarms haven't started blaring yet.

Taking matters into your own hands, you sprint around the counter and quickly struggle to understand the mechanics of this large industrial grill. Seconds later you find the heat switch and turn it off, then run over and grab a set of tongs that are hanging nearby. You take the charred remains of the burger and pick it up from the sizzling hot grill, bringing it over and dropping it in the sink.

You turn on the cool water and watch as steam plumes up with a loud hiss.

It takes a moment for you to collect your senses, but once you do you realize that something is very wrong. Ben must be in trouble.

"Hello?" you call out. "Is anyone here? The food was burning!"

There's no response at all, and the silence is strangely haunting. You stand for a while, frozen in place as you listen for any sign of life. Beyond this front section of the establishment is the door to the prep kitchen in back, a place that would be great to explore if it weren't for the strange, disturbing smell that's currently emanating from its recesses.

The burning burger had been enough to hide this bizarre toxic aroma, but now that the food has been taken care of, brand new information begins to waft across your nostrils.

The scent is hard to pin down, and although parts of it seem completely foreign, there's something about it that's distinctly unpleasant in an almost primal way. It smells toxic.

Suddenly, a voice cuts through the silence, emanating from the prep kitchen in back.

"It's me, Ben! Everything is just fine," a voice calls out. "Come on back, there's a new recipe I'm working on."

Go back and see Ben on page 74

It seems like this place isn't safe, let's head to The Chocolate Milk Man on page 65

It seems like this place isn't safe, let's head to The Spaghetti Hut on page 75

It seems like this place isn't safe, let's head to the mall's central hub on page 9

Printed in Great Britain
by Amazon